Interruption

Robin Densmore Fuson

BROKEN YOKE
PUBLISHING

Praise for Interruption

In the tradition of Lewis, Robin Densmore Fuson brings us the flipside of the Screwtape letters. This very thoughtful work of speculative, theologically sound, fiction asks the question: How can our guardian angels keep our feet from "dashing against a stone" (Ps 91:11-12) while still allowing our character to be developed through trials (James 1:2-5; Rom 5:3-5); not to mention still experience the consequences for our sin (Gal 6:7; Eph 4:30). I do not want to give anything away, but I have been preaching for 30 years and I kept thinking, as I was reading, "Why hadn't I thought of that?"

You need to read this book! It will encourage your heart and sharpen your walk.

> Pastor Scott Sundin
> Word of Grace Fellowship
> Kansas City MO

I found Interruption somewhere between Frank Peretti's books and Pilgrim's Progress. I love Robin's descriptions. Her words came alive. The characters were real, especially the All-Knowing One, who I felt closer to as the story progressed. Very good book, one I highly recommend.

Randy Tramp, Author of Night to Knight.

Robin Densmore Fuson's book, "Interruption" is the

perfect interruption in Christian fiction. An easy read that allows you to parallel your life to the main character, Jacquelyn. Whether you have physically experienced a second chance at life or you view embracing the newness of life Christ provides us through salvation, it will speak to you in such positive ways!

Pastor Katherine S. Ferry
Children's Pastor

I dedicate this story to the One who gave me the idea of *Interruption* and guided me step by step through the process, Jesus Christ, the Commander of the Lord's Army, the Lord of Hosts. Thank you, Father, for sending Your Son to save my wretched self and for gifting me in imagination and storytelling.

Hebrews 13:2 Don't forget to show hospitality to strangers, for some who have done this have entertained angels without realizing it!

Mathew 18:10 Beware that you don't look down on any of these little ones. For I tell you that in heaven their angels are always in the presence of my heavenly Father.

Ephesians 6:10-12 A final word: Be strong in the Lord and in his mighty power. Put on all of God's armor so that you will be able to stand firm against all strategies of the devil. For we are not fighting against flesh-and-blood enemies, but against evil rulers and authorities of the unseen world, against mighty powers in this dark world, and against evil spirits in the heavenly places.

Chapter 1

1957
Jacquelyn

I remember the time I died, as if, you know, as if it happened yesterday. Thank the Lord, it didn't. Yesterday, I figured out why the Lord gave me a second chance at life.

Faphick

"I, Faphick, Guardian of Jacquelyn Carter, do swear to protect and guard her in the keeping of the rules set forth from the Throne of God on High."

I pummeled my chest as I bowed. Yes, this promise I understood and would do anything to fulfill. As part of my duties, I would give account to my Sovereign Lord of Hosts of what I witnessed and how I intervened.

As I made my way to the armory, the normal questions rattled through my brain. Would this baby, yet to be welcomed into the earthly realm, be a special creation garnered with exceptional capacity and calling, or a life steady yet uneventful? I raised my brow. Did the female's destiny involve sorrow, pain, and tragedy? How many times would I need to intervene?

The orders were clear but the details of how to obey remained unclear as always. I knew from experience those would flood my mind at the moment when needed—never too early but never after the fact. God on High knew all and dispensed needed information at the exact moment.

Other Valiant Ones stood in line to take possession of the weapons and equipment needed for their jobs. The array seemed endless, for each human needed individual care and their circumstances would warrant special equipment. Each of us always carried our unique sword given to us at our creation before God created the human domain. At that time, we also received our title and rank. A special helmet, footgear, breastplate, and shield for the purpose of strength and honor, never left us. Those, as well as we, represented the One we served and Who enabled us and gave us power.

Being a Valiant One was an honored position. Never would I desire a different station. I stepped forward and accepted the vital tools. The apparatus needed for my new assignment fit securely into my Belt of Truth. I fastened my glistening white robe overtop and took off to my post as Guardian of Jacquelyn Carter—watchful and ready for anything.

1952
Fifteen-year-old Jacquelyn

My dance classes paid off and I've been dancing professionally since I turned ten. All those years ago, Mom came with me to Denver from my birthplace of Grand Junction to be my chaperone. An amazing adventure for a ten-year-old to climb aboard the bus not knowing the long, boring hours that awaited my impatient heart. Mom tried to keep me occupied but I'd rather tap my feet up and down the aisle, I'm sure, to my mother's frustration. Most people were cool about it, smiling encouragement.

1947
Ten-year-old Jacquelyn

One man called out, "Kid, you are no Ginger Rogers. Give us some peace and quiet. Lady, can't you give her some knock-out powder or something?"

Mom grabbed me and held me tightly on her lap. "Jackie, sit here and rest for a while until I say you can get up."

Darkness descended. A confined position and the whine of the tires on pavement lulled me to sleep. At least I don't think Mom gave me anything in the orange juice she had me drink. The jerk of the bus coming to a halt woke me and we took our turn in line to climb down. Fumes made me wrinkle my nose. I kept close to my mom as people crowded. Mom handed a man our baggage claim ticket. She retrieved our borrowed luggage and handed me the small one. "Jackie, stay with me."

I followed on her heels as she meandered through the throng of people. I didn't know where to look—too many things sparkled, moved, or made noise. Never had I been in such a large building. Benches sat row upon row. The polished floor caught my attention. "Oh my!" My feet itched to tap a rhythm across that shiny floor. Mom jerked her head for me to speed up. "Keep up, Jackie."

I followed my mom through a door that pushed me to go into a circle and I almost didn't get out in time. "Aah!" I stumbled forward and turned to watch as it spat others out.

"Are you all right?"

I nodded.

"That's a revolving door. It's designed to keep the weather out and the people moving. No need for a doorman. Come on, we need to find a cab." She led me to the line of yellow cars where an empty one waited. A skinny guy got out and dumped our bags into the trunk and I crawled up on the back seat next to Mom. After we left the station, the buildings rose like giants on each side. I pressed my nose to the window, trying to catch sight of everything at once.

"Why are they so tall?"

"Many people live and work here. Most are office buildings or stores."

Buildings back home were much shorter and there were not as many people, cars, and trucks. Horns blew as cars sped by.

The motel's neon vacancy sign pointed to the place we would call home. Mom gave the woman some money, signed her name in a book, and got a key. The room with two beds welcomed us. I ran to one, claiming it for my own.

5

Interruption

I slipped out my one comfort from home, Dorothy, my doll, and propped her onto my pillow, straightening her hair. "Sweet Dorothy, are you glad to get out of the bag? This is our new home. What do you think?"

Having had my nap on the bus, I wanted to explore. "Mom, can we take a walk? You said there were stores. Can we at least look in the windows?"

Mom handed me a book. "Read. You need to rest. Audition is first thing in the morning. And this is not a place to explore at night."

She tossed me my nightgown and we both readied ourselves for bed.

Brush in hand, she sat beside me and detangled the mess of my hair. "Your hair is the color of coal but glistening and smooth. You take after your father—the feminine to his masculine. He was a handsome man. Though tall, he had a strong and muscular build, intelligent gray eyes, and was stubborn like you." She hugged me. "So much like him. He could have been a dancer or anything else he wanted. Nevertheless, he did what his father and grandfather did, and too soon, the mines took him."

Mom kissed my forehead. "Get some sleep." She switched off the overhead light and I watched the lights play across the ceiling from every passing car and thought about a father I never met. Often at home, I had looked at the photograph of Mom and Dad that sat on the mantel over the fireplace, where I had memorized his face. Mom had slipped it into her suitcase before we left and I wished I had taken it out to hold to my chest.

Faphick

Tiny Jacquelyn came into the world screaming. Her cry made me smile. Good. A fighter with healthy lungs. My cursory glance showed a healthy baby. The crowded room held people tending to her and her mother and more than a dozen spirit Beings, each with an agenda. Beings who stood with the Captain of the Lord of Hosts wanted the best for this child, but the fallen angels wanted to destroy this freshly born person. This must be a special one to have so many after her short life.

Jackie's first few years moved through time rather quickly, at least in my experience. I shrugged. The occasional person sickness and falls with scraped knees and elbows. Her feet were the most impressive ones I've had the honor to protect. The Lord on High gave her a special ability that the humans treasure. Dance.

The little family of two, accompanied by Xamiel, Jackie's mother's Guardian, and myself, boarded a bus for Denver. The compartment teemed with people and spirits. Xamiel and I had our work cut out for us. Jackie's antics, although harmless and adorable, elicited hostility from some people and Beings encouraged the sentiments. One person listened to Malicious, a spirit Being, and blurted out what others thought. Finally, Mrs. Carter pulled Jackie on her lap and I wrapped my arms around them both and whispered the song I always sang to calm my young charge. All the while, busy Xamiel kept a semblance of peace.

The bus stopped and Xamiel and I accompanied them as they worked their way to the terminal. I smiled as I watched Jackie's awe of the place. Beings swarmed around her and tried to dislodge her footing. She tried to see everything all at once and would have tripped a few times but I guided her feet.

Leaving the building, there might have been a mishap. As Jackie entered the revolving door, Mayhem and Impatience crowded into her space. I zoomed in to lift her and set her on the pavement outside the revolving door. Otherwise, they intended to use the door behind to push her, causing injury.

After we were safe inside the cab, I replayed the scene and chuckled. Children, well, people, have no clue as to how many times we help them out of danger. Yes, sometimes we let them fall but most of the time we intervene. Troubles, sicknesses, and injuries help form people into what they need to become. Out of love for His creation, the Lord on High allows these lessons, and the Valiant Ones stand down.

Jacquelyn

Morning came too soon. Mom took me to the facilities down the hall and gave me a good cleansing, even scrubbing behind my ears. Why that would make me dance better, I had no idea. I squirmed and fought like any kid.

We walked the mile to the theater, stopping along the route for some breakfast. People and cars grabbed my attention. Mom took my hand. "Don't dawdle."

We entered a place to eat with red booths and tables sitting on a black and white checkered floor. Music blared and I wanted to tap to the beat.

A lady smacking gum between her bright teeth took our order. I glanced all around trying to memorize the place and the people. Mom didn't seem to mind my gawking, as she called it. After a while, the gum lady slid our plates in front of us. Mom said grace and I scooped up my first bite. Boy, did those eggs and toast taste good. I'd never eaten at a diner before. The smells, taste, music, people's faces and voices, and the clattering of dishes would be forever burned into my mind. Mom cut my portions in half. "Eat this much. Too full of a stomach will make you sick."

I frowned.

"Don't worry, I'll give you the rest after your auditions. You like egg sandwiches." She piled the egg onto the toast and wrapped it in napkins. Pulling out a piece of waxed paper from her purse, she covered it and placed it into the bag that held everything imaginable. I had a great imagination and the black imposing thing frightened yet intrigued me.

Around the block, Mom ushered me into the theater. The huge stage almost took my breath. I'd not seen one so big nor so high off the ground. I gulped air. The auditorium's floor floated up and away from the stage, holding what seemed like millions of chairs in straight lines facing the empty black space. Heavy black curtains made the backdrop and skimmed the scuffed, immense black floor.

Down front, I sat next to other children and waited for my turn. Mom had returned to the back to get a good view, where other parents waited. I felt their tension from here. The crossed arms and expressionless faces of the adults as Mom took an empty seat made me glad I stayed here with the kids.

I took another deep breath—I had to do this alone. I pulled my tap shoes from the bag I had carried with me. I yanked off my outside shoes and slipped on the black shiny dance ones over my white laced ankle socks.

Interruption

One by one, the kids were called onto the stage and showed their routines. One girl made me want to punch her. She held her head up with her nose in the air and flung her hair back over her shoulder. The twit's skinny legs flew, slamming her shoes against the floor, tapping staccato with the music they played. When the music stopped, she curtsied! Curtsied as if she had to impress the Princess of Egypt or Pharaoh himself. I knew enough Bible stories to see where this was going. She sashayed (I liked that word) herself back down to her chair and gave the rest of us the evil eye before smiling sweetly to the people who would choose four of us for the roles we were competing for.

A cute boy with a silly grin did a fine job and I hoped he made it. The rest I didn't care about one way or the other as long as I got in, of course. After all, we came from such a long way and Mom had her heart set on it. The pressure made me squirm.

"Jacquelyn Carter." I jerked to attention. The lady called my name. I stood and went over to the stairs. My hands felt wet so I wiped them on my short skirt. I needed to win a slot on this show. Aunt Sherry had slipped Mom money for this trip. With no dad, Mom worked hard to pay for my dance lessons and she said she had dreams for me. I just hoped I could make her dreams come true. I took another deep breath and let it slowly out as I climbed the stairs.

Faphick

Jacquelyn squared her shoulders and nodded for the music to start. Her heart raced and I sensed Fear but I saw the gleam of determination. I clanged my sword against Fear's and, with her tamping that emotion down, Fear backed off. Jackie's feet zipped and flipped. I slashed my sword in a swirling arc all around her. No Being would trip my charge. The energy created by all the players would have powered the largest man-made city for six days. After this was over at some point, I hope God on High will let me see how she did.

The music ended and the Beings left her alone. I relaxed and peered at her over my shoulder. Her little self made me proud. She finished and smiled at her judges and skipped down to take her seat. In a blink, I hugged her and whispered, "Fine job. We are all proud of you and all the hard work you put in."

1952
Fifteen-year-old Jacquelyn

I won a slot in the musical and for the next five years, we trudged across the country where I played bit parts or sometimes the lead in musicals and plays. I got to the point where I didn't need my mom and made it clear. "Mom, go live with Aunt Sherry. I can take care of myself. Anyway, I signed on with the troupe and I'll be traveling with them on the bus. They don't have their moms with them. Moms aren't allowed and I don't need you following. Anyhow, you're causing a stir. For cryin' out loud, I'm fifteen! You've got my schedule. How about meeting, say, next Christmas in California?"

I'd made up my mind and no amount of persuasion would change it. I expected tears to trail down her cheeks but she smiled bravely and hugged me tightly. "Please write and I'll keep track of you from the papers. Telegraph the postmaster if you need me. I love you!"

"Love you too and don't worry. You're lucky. You'll get to sleep on a regular bed and eat home-cooked meals. I'll be fine. You'll see."

I didn't get to meet Mom for Christmas. Cancer took her away. I never saw her beautiful face again or felt her arms around me.

Faphick

I knew I had nothing to do with her success but I felt proud. Throughout the formative years, Jackie's mom made sure her girl went to church as often as possible and Xamiel and I circled them. Years ago, Jackie's seven-year-old heart heard about her Creator and how He loved her so much that He sent His only Son to die for her. Every time I was reminded about the day Christ died, thousands of years ago in human terms, I almost exploded with praise! The God-ordained day etched itself in my mind. The sadness might have killed us as we watched Jesus Christ go through the terrible brutality and then die. We Valiant Ones and angels had orders to stand down no matter what happened. So dark. So evil. Excruciating. No other event made me cry like that. I still don't understand all that is involved in the reason God's Son had to die so brutally.

Silence from the Throne. We thought He would stop it. I looked up into the heavens expecting the Father to give the word. We were ready. All I knew was the silence. When He turned away from His Son, it almost took me to my knees. Even the fallen ones stood still. Christ, all alone, died in agony.

God's will had to be done. All of it, for humanity.

I rejoice now because Jesus Christ didn't stay dead! No. God raised Himself from the grave after waiting an earthly three days. Hallelujah! So, when I think back to that day, I can praise and sing and dance for joy!

But, back to my charge. She understood what Christ did for her and she accepted His payment for her sin. She was God's child now—a new creation. The Holy Spirit resided in Jackie's spirit.

I thought my battles to protect her would let up. Unfortunately, no. The treasure I guarded would soon endure sadness and pain. I wanted to shield her from it all but God on High expected me to let her stumble and hurt. God made people with a free will like us. I chose long ago on Whose side I stood. Now, my girl had to make those choices. She was God's but how she would live was still up to her.

Jackie danced and sang on stage all over the country. Her proud mom beamed with delight and fussed over her. This mother loved her girl more than many other moms loved their children.

Gradually, a change came over Jackie. Independence. I had to stand by and do nothing when she all but tossed her mom out of her life. Jackie welcomed and embraced Independence and Pride.

Interruption

Xamiel left Earth with Jackie's mom and my girl had only her traveling troupe for companionship. I knew she missed her mom and she seemed lonely. She marked off days on her calendar and a red circle marked the day her mom would meet her in California.

A sinking feeling came over me when Xamiel came. Jackie took the telegram from the motel manager. "Thank you." She opened the page and read. The paper slipped from her hand. I put my arm around her as she fell and I guided her to the floor.

Comprehension flooded me.

Xamiel put his hand on my shoulder. "I came to be with you and Jackie as soon as her aunt sent the dispatch. Her mother had known she had cancer when she left but she didn't want to disrupt Jackie's assignment. Her mother is enjoying Heaven. I need to get back there, I have a new commission. This time my assignment is a male to guard."

We embraced and he zipped away. I sat on the floor and cried with young Jackie, who thought she was all alone in the world.

Chapter 2

1953
Jacquelyn

I went into the skids. I missed Mom. I had no one but the troupe. "Orphan" rang through my heart and mind. I never knew my dad. He died in a mining accident when I still teetered on two-year-old legs. Mom cleaned houses and took in ironing to support us. She said I always danced. My feet tapped out rhythms before I took my first steps. She sold everything that wasn't necessary and worked from sun-up to late in the night to pay for my classes, shoes, and outfits. How did she know I loved to dance and would never want to do anything else?

The rigors of rehearsals, short stays in strange places with not enough sleep, lousy food, and poor company brought disastrous decisions.

Alcohol grabbed me. The demons got louder until pills were added to the mix. Luckily, I didn't smoke. Although, the glamorous women in the movies looked so sophisticated blowing smoke in a guy's face. I took pills to sleep and pills to wake and to keep up with the other dancers. The dropping weight caused a necessity to pin my outfits. Barely making it in my dance numbers, I took more uppers, drank more coffee, and ate sugary foods.

I'm not sure how I lasted as long as I did.

Faphick

Jackie's self-destruction came slow and steady. My commission and my oath demanded that I do nothing to stop her decline. She had a will and choices she made all by herself. Spirits taunted and tempted her. I did as much as I had permission to do. When she let the bad influences affect her, I could do nothing against them. I kept the others away whom she had not invited. I wept for her and with her. I sang to her. I walked each day with her and watched over her all the time. God on High saw, felt, and knew each moment and all the future. I rested in that knowledge. He loved her.

God on High let me know when the time drew near. I understood what unfolded before me.

Soon.

1954
Chicago, IL
Jacquelyn

I felt nothing. My body jerked. Noises and voices seemed to fade. I became aware that I looked down on myself lying on a gurney. Odd. People scurried around me as one man pounded his fist on my chest in a rhythm and took time to blow into my mouth. I floated up and away.

At once, I stood on luxurious grass trimmed and well maintained—the color of the most vibrant shamrock green. The lawn felt exceptionally soft under my bare feet. My toes curled in anticipation of immersion in the velvet texture. The air around me—light and fragrant. I closed my eyes as I inhaled the cleanness and wiggled my feet in the turf.

A noise captured my attention. In the purest turquoise azure sky I have ever seen flew a large hawk overhead and the sound I'd heard seemed to come from him. A melodic bell chord sang forth from him signaling his arrival to the top of an extremely full tree laden with fruit. The fruit I didn't recognize burdened the tree branches, causing them to drape toward the ground. No fruit had fallen. The pristine landscape held no touch of disturbance.

Past the tree, I saw a magnificently carved gate that sparkled in its radiance. Drawn to the gate, my feet thanked me as I padded across the expanse. The gate swung open in a slow arc without so much as a whisper. The grass carpet continued through the entrance and I accepted the invitation. Impressive flowers in more than every shade of the rainbow smiled their faces toward me. People roamed singly, or in groups, and pairs. Some bent to take in the fragrance of a close bloom. A woman tucked a bright red beauty behind the ear of a child—exquisite against her dark flowing hair. The murmur of voices comforted me. Smiles and waves greeted me and I felt accepted.

Ahead, a golden walkway wound up a hill. I wondered where it led and took a few steps. A warm clasp of my shoulder caused me to stop and turn. A tall, well-built man stood beside me. The beautifully handsome face smiled down at me. Love radiated from the most compassionate and kind eyes I'd ever encountered. Instinct told me I could trust Him as if my life depended on Him.

"Come walk with me." His voice, deep and rich, like a harp on the low strings, vibrated over me.

I wanted to weep. I nodded. His arm slipped across my shoulders as we went to the walkway. I glanced down at

His powerful hand and noticed a deep scar in the middle. The sight of it made me feel amazingly comforted. The walkway waited for us, shaded by trees and flowers that grew at its borders. Light glinted off the surface as if they were made from gold. The pavers were warm and smooth yet I knew I'd not slip or fall.

I bent to smell and touch a giant purple blossom. A heady fragrance swam through my senses. I caressed the petal's satiny softness—as smooth as a newborn baby's cheek.

We walked a while and came to a bridge over a river. At the center of the bridge, we stopped. The water flowed over rocks and boulders. The babble came to my ears like the belly laugh of an infant. I giggled.

He joined me.

"The melody is beautiful. A few people want to greet you." He turned slightly. "Ah, here they come now." He swept His hand to the far side of the bridge. A large group ranging in age walked toward me. Smiles radiated from them.

I felt like I must know them. I frowned up at the man. "I know them?"

"Yes. They are ones you love and love you."

I turned with expectancy. "Hello."

One by one they embraced me and I knew them—their names so easy on my tongue. Grandma and Grandpa Carter, Grandma and Grandpa Duke, aunts, uncles, cousins, great-grandparents, great uncles and aunts, both older and also children I never knew but yet did. I wondered at the pleasure. They kept coming—each hug special and generous. My whole being felt the love radiate from them. Elation enveloped me as my momma cupped my face. "Baby, what a gift to behold your face. I want you to know I'm proud of you and all you accomplished. You've done amazing things with the talent the Lord gave you. I'm partial to who you are inside and what wonderful things you will still accomplish."

She rested her hand on my heart and searched my eyes. "Honey, please tell your Aunt Sherry I love her and we will spend eternity together here with our Lord."

Joyfulness almost burst into a song, I felt so happy. My momma was more beautiful than I remembered and smiled at me.

"Momma."

Her arms encircled me and I rested my head against her shoulder. Warmth and love flowed from the embrace.

After a time, she stepped back but kept her hands on my arms. "I speak for all of us. We are so blessed to have had this moment with you. Always remember, we love you and are so proud of you. However, no one loves you as much as our Lord does." Her hands slipped to clasp mine and she looked up past me to my companion.

Momma hugged me again. "Never forget and never lose heart. Keep moving forward even when the way seems impossible."

She patted my cheek and turned toward the group. I watched them make their way back to where they had come. I couldn't help the immense grin. A peaceful bliss flooded me. My people—the ones who loved me.

"Jacquelyn."

My name swirled around me like a caress. I turned to my guide. A huge smile graced His face.

"Yes?"

"Journey with me." He guided me back the way we had come, only this time under the laden trees. He reached for a fruit. "Here, refresh yourself."

I grinned and took the proffered plump magenta fruit. I sunk my teeth into the firm flesh and was rewarded by a tantalizing rich flavor yet with a hint of tang to the sweetness. Unbelievable goodness swirled around my mouth. So perfect a flavor, I delighted in every bite. Refresh it did and satisfied my taste buds as well as my stomach. I figured I'd never need to eat again.

"I'm glad you enjoyed your food." His kind smile warmed me.

"Jacquelyn, you cannot stay right now. You need to go back, for I have work for you to do. I will go with you and help you, never to forsake you. All you have to do is call on me. You won't see me but my presence is always there.

Interruption

Trust me. Lean into me and trust my understanding of the way before you. Acknowledge me in all you do. Sweet Jacquelyn, remember when you were seven and trusted me as your Lord? The Comforter lives in you and has been and will be, your helper. I'm there with you and also commune with the Father on your behalf. Oh, how He loves you! He and I talk about you and delight in you. Your job on Earth is not complete. Trust Us through the changes and stages that will happen."

I nodded, eager to do whatever He asked me to do.

"I have a special man in mind for you. He will come to enrich your life. Your future is bright. There will be hard times and sadness but We will get you through. All you need to do is trust Us."

So much had happened. I felt secure in all I had learned and experienced. I didn't mourn as we walked back. How could I? Exaltation, elation, ecstasy, love, and all the immense delightful emotions flowed through every corpuscle of my being.

He hugged me, bringing a warmth I had never experienced. Part of me wanted to beg to stay but I knew the best thing would be to leave. He had given me a job, something important.

"Child, I wait for you and am preparing a special dwelling for you when the time is right. Be patient but live with expectancy."

Back on the bed, the jumbled voices came to me, and pain shot through my body.

Faphick

Driving and alcohol were a dangerous combination. The driver died when the car hit the tree. The passengers had different degrees of injuries. I held Jackie through the crash, while we waited for help, and when they tried to revive her all three times. The third time, I got the orders to take her to Heaven. This part was always the best. I stayed at the gate of Heaven as she made her way inside.

I waited.

Not yet her turn to stay, I took her back to Earth. God on High had more for this woman to do—an important mission. I was ecstatic for her.

Chapter 3

1955
Jacquelyn

Rehab was extremely difficult. At first, I fought the doctors and staff. Then I resigned myself to work and get well. The withdrawal from drugs and alcohol felt excruciating but month by month I healed. My physical injuries left scars.

One night, a dream became a memory of my time in Heaven. I woke up crying. Heaven. This had happened. I knew it did. I determined I would find out more about the time I died.

After days of a run-around, the admin representative called me to her office. "We told Dr. Smith that you haven't been sleeping, fretting over the night you were in emergency. Although he is a busy man, he said will call you as soon as he could. I shouldn't give you his number but I know you will bother me until he calls." She held the paper. "Promise you will give him three days to call."

I reached for the page.

She pulled it away. "Promise."

"I promise." I crossed my heart. "Three days. But, only three."

I held the paper and impatiently walked back to my room.

The phone in my room rang. "Hello?"

"Jacquelyn Carter?"

"Yes."

"This is Dr. Smith. Can you meet with me at ten on Thursday?"

I glanced at my scheduled appoints and sessions. "Yes, that will work."

"I'll meet you in the courtyard."

"Sure. All right, see you then. Dr. Smith, thank you for calling." I hung up. I stared at the paper snug in my grip and smoothed it out before placing it my datebook. Now I only had to get through until Thursday.

Faphick

Again, Jackie pulled her knees up, wrapped her arms around them, laid her head down, and rocked. This had become an all too familiar scene when alone in her room. She stayed in this position, rocking, until she finally succumbed to sleep and toppled over. My songs didn't help but I sang through every night, through her bad dreams, through the torture of her mind and body. I did what God on High allowed.

Loneliness, Despair, Worry, and Heartache pestered her. Depression shrouded her like a cloud covers a mountain. She had let them influence her thoughts. Beings can only wreak havoc with the mind, will, and emotions of believers who have put their faith and trust in Jesus Christ as Lord. They cannot occupy their spirit where the Holy Spirit dwells. They cannot take up residence.

The treatment for drug abuse seemed to be working. The sweats, tremors, and moaning through the night might have caused me to worry had I not known the Lord on High went through it with her. He let me do what I could. Her body experienced terrible withdrawals. If only her mind and emotions could heal as swiftly.

Then one night her dream changed from nightmare to peace. Her time in Heaven replayed in her subconscious and she relaxed into a deep, uninterrupted, peaceful sleep.

She awoke, stretched, and jumped out of bed. She opened the blinds for the first time since she had moved in. Loneliness, Despair, Worry, Heartache, and Depression had been replaced by Peace and Calm.

Jackie called and asked for the doctor who she thought had resuscitated her.

Every day she called and after appealing in person, finally got his name. She held tight to the paper with his phone number. When she got to her room, her phone rang. I heard the doctor invite her to meet him in the courtyard and he would bring coffee.

The facility she lived in had everything she needed physically but, emotionally and spiritually, it lacked or, rather, did nothing to fill the void. I knew Who she needed. He waited with a listening ear as patient as the Ancient of Days always is, was, and will be.

Jacquelyn

A slight breeze rustled the leaves in the tree above the bench where I waited for Doctor Smith. I came twenty minutes early to get the only bench and keep others away. A man who appeared to be in his thirties, carrying a basket, came over. As I was about to tell him to leave, he said, "Miss Carter, you look much better than the last time I saw you. Doctor Smith, at your service." He reached out his hand. I took it—warm, firm, and reassuring.

"It's nice to meet you. Please sit down."

Interruption

He sat and opened the basket. "I hope you like cream and sugar. I brought a thermos of coffee and cups. I figured a glazed doughnut might be acceptable too."

He smiled at me and I couldn't help but grin back. "Thank you. Before you pour the coffee, please tell me what happened that night."

"Sure." He placed the basket on his other side. "I came upon the scene right after the crash. Did they tell you about that part?"

"I remember Danny swerving and the car headed straight to the tree. I screamed and that's the last I remember."

"The car hit the tree head on. The driver..." He studied my face. "Danny died immediately. I opened the door to the back seat and checked all the occupants' pulses. I pulled each one out and administered care. You were the worst. A tree limb had gone through the windshield, missing the front passenger."

"Judy."

"Judy."

"Stan and Joey were in the back with me. I sat between them."

"That's how I found you." He reached up and touched the place on my head. "You've healed nicely."

I forced a smile. "Seems strange to have a tree smack someone in the head and the heart at the same time."

He nodded. "That tree did a number on you. I'm glad I arrived when I did. The blow to your head brought on extensive bleeding, but the blow to your chest caused Commotio Cordis. Your heart stopped. I used a new procedure James Otis Elam had introduced—rescue breathing and closed chest compression. I had read about it in a journal that very day. You, my dear, are the first one I resuscitated—three times, too."

I couldn't believe it. "Three?"

"I'm afraid so, once before the ambulance got there. Someone must have called the hospital. You are a lucky girl."

"I thought you were with me in the hospital?"

"Right." He nodded. "I never left your side. I forced my way into the ambulance. They didn't want me. I told them I was a doctor and I had restarted your heart and no one would keep me from going to make sure it kept beating. They had never heard of such a thing so I had a fight on my hands. You were too important for me to neglect. By God's will, I stayed with you until He and you decided to stay with us. On the way, your heart failed again. I brought it back under control. Everything appeared to be fine then as soon as we transferred you to a bed in the hospital, your heart stopped again. I feverishly worked on you. They told me to quit.

"As God is my witness, I had brought you back before and I just couldn't quit. They called the time of your death and were cleaning up the room as I kept pumping on your chest and blowing in your mouth to give you air. You, my dear, are a miracle. After twelve minutes, you came back. Your heart beat by itself and that steady rhythm has been going on since."

"A miracle." My mind went to that room as I floated away. "I died. I remember going to Heaven."

"Interesting. Let me pour you some coffee and you can tell me about your experience."

The perfect coffee caressed my tongue and the doughnut melted in my mouth. Nothing had ever tasted so good. "How did you know how I liked my coffee?"

He shrugged. "I have a confession, I called here and asked."

"Thank you. It's been a long time since someone did something special for me."

"Did your family set you up here?" He waved his hand toward the building where I lived.

My stomach contracted. "I don't have immediate family. My Aunt Sherry worked it out. I really didn't want to be here, but now, I'm all right with the rules and the sermons."

"Sermons?"

"Mrs. White modeled this treatment facility after one that started in Boston. The Emanuel movement started in a church. I don't know much about it."

He nodded. "I see. Would you like another doughnut? You should have more than one because today is National Doughnut Day."

I grinned. "I'd love one. The food here isn't very good." I reached into the basket and pulled out another gooey pastry.

"So, tell me what happened. You said you went to Heaven?"

I immediately recalled my dream. I knew I had a silly grin but I couldn't help it. The place. The experience. How did I explain?

"Jackie, what do you remember first?"

"I floated." I swallowed. That sounded weird even to my ears. "Yes, I floated up above and I saw myself on the bed with you bending over me. So very strange. Then, all of a sudden, I stood on luxurious grass. Nothing I'd ever felt before. The textures, smell, sounds, and exceptional beauty tantalized my senses. I don't know how to describe everything. Unimaginable.

"Huge trees." I spread out my arms, mimicking a large circle. "Giant blooms of flowers in so many different colors, some I'd never seen before, were everywhere and all well maintained. The grounds seemed to be designed and ordered. Oh!" I couldn't help my excitement. "I saw my family. Everyone. Great, great, greats I never met, I somehow knew." My hands flew to my face cupping my

33

cheeks. "My momma! Momma so pretty, kissed me and held me."

"That must have been wonderful. Did she talk to you?"

"She said she loved me and was proud of me. To never lose heart and keep moving forward."

"What else do you remember?"

"Him. The man who met me and showed me around and sent me back. Him."

"Who was he?"

"I believe, He must be Jesus. So kind. So tender to me. Strong. Beautiful. He made me feel precious and special even more than Momma did. I will never forget His eyes. Warmth and compassion wrapped around me when He looked upon me. My words do not describe how I felt. I trusted Him completely and wanted to do anything He asked. He told me to go back because He had more for me to do. What do you suppose that means?"

Dr. Smith rested his hand on the back of mine. "Only you can answer that. Pray about it. Have you talked with anyone else about this?"

I shook my head.

He removed his hand. "Do you meet with anyone from the counseling psychology field to talk about your life?"

"Only a few times. Mrs. White insists on a session every few weeks. I'm scheduled to be released soon."

"Are you worried about that? Have you plans?"

I shrugged. "I've tried not to think about it."

"What about your aunt?"

I shrugged again. "She lives in Colorado."

"Did you contact her for suggestions?" He had an uncanny way of looking deep into my eyes as if he could read my thoughts. "What did you do before the accident?"

"I performed. I'm a dancer. I belonged to a troupe but they filled my slot. They quit answering my letters and calls." I shrugged. I seemed to be doing that a lot lately. Why did God say He had plans for me when I didn't have a job or a place to live? I jumped up. "Thank you for coming and answering my question. Oh, and the coffee and doughnuts." I put out my hand.

He took it as he stood. "It was nice seeing you again. I'm glad you are well. Call your aunt." He lifted his shoulders. "What can it hurt?" He let go of my hand.

I turned and almost ran to my room, shut the door, and fell onto my bed. The tears racked my body.

Chapter 4

Faphick

I felt her tension. At first, Jackie seemed relaxed in the doctor's company and enjoyed reminiscing about Heaven but as soon as the doctor brought up counseling and her future, a switched seemed to have flipped. Agitation and Fear tormented her. She abruptly ended her conversation. She acted as if something chased her. Did she sense the ones who did?

Dr. Smith's Guardian and I were kept busy protecting these two people from interruptions, darts, and jabs. Fear, a huge enemy who always hovered near, pounced as soon as she let him. Agitation pushed against Fear and they fought to churn her emotions. I had to stand down from that scrimmage because she had let them come. Others scurried near trying to get an invitation. Those I kept back with my sword. All the way to her room and through the next few days, the battle waged.

Jacquelyn

I felt miserable. I was so tired but I had to find a place to live. I only had three days. With no other option, I called Aunt Sherry. What if she didn't want me? What if she couldn't help? What would I do? I had no money and no job. My weight had fallen off from my healthy days when Mom had been around. I didn't keep up my exercise and dance. To be honest, I hadn't opened the box that the troupe sent me which had my outfits and shoes, not wanting to face it.

I heard her phone ring and ring and ring. Aloud to my room, I pretended she answered as I heard the insufferable ringing. "Aunt Sherry, this is Jackie. My time at Mrs. White's is almost over. I don't know where to go. The troupe won't hire me back." My voice broke. I held back my tears and cleared my throat.

I hung up the unanswered phone and plopped on the bed. The dammed-up tears broke. I was all alone. I didn't have a job. My friends with the troupe abandoned me. What was I going to do? I jumped up and paced back and forth in my cube of a room from door to window and back.

There has to be something. Oh boy, did I want a drink. Only a little one to take the edge off. The more I thought of it the faster I walked, back and forth, back and forth. I bit my lip. There was no one to care for me. I had nobody. I fell on my bed and sobbed.

Faphick

Many spirits invaded her quarters. No rest for me in sight. Poor, agitated, fearful Jackie stomped and raged at the way life had treated her. Fear and Agitation cheered, pushed, and pulled her. Temptation flung vices at her and her flesh clasped his hand. Dependency spoke over the noise swaying her to need him. Keeping my sword arching to keep the others away, I backed into her to knock her on the bed. Tears came, relieving some of the pressure. How much more would she need to endure?

Jacquelyn

A knock at my door caused me to hold my breath and listen. Go Away, I wanted to shout. The sound came again. "Jackie. Are you there? It's Aunt Sherry."

What? I felt paralyzed.

The doorknob turned and the door opened. In she waltzed with a huge smile. "There you are. Oh, honey, what's the matter?"

In a blink, she had me in her arms and rocked me. Nothing had felt so good. My body relaxed but the tears kept up their trek down my face and dripped onto her arms.

When I could control my crying, I mumbled, "How? I just called you but you didn't answer. How could you? You were on your way here. How did you know?"

"Honey, I get reports on your wellbeing and progress every week. I knew the time came to take you home. We leave tomorrow. A train will take us across the country and over the mountains, home. The train ride will help you get into a different routine and some uninterrupted rest if you need it and amazing scenery will bolster you. We have a sleeper car with a huge window. You can stay in there the whole trip or visit the dining car or observation car. This will be a mini vacation. There are stops along the way too. Are you hungry?"

I nodded. Too much to take in. A train? She came to take me home to Grand Junction? Home. She called it home. For me too?

"How about a pizza?"

"What's that?"

"Let's go find out. Go wash your face and I'll take you to a restaurant that boasts, 'Best Pizza in the World.' We won't know because we have nothing to compare it to but it sounds like a lovely adventure." She squeezed me tight and then pulled me to my feet, giving me a pat of encouragement as she sent me out the door to the washroom down the hall.

"Ready?" she asked when I slipped back into the room.

She had made my bed and folded the clothes I had in the laundry basket. Just like Mom. I smiled. "Thanks."

"You don't need to thank me." She linked her arm through mine and we went out to a cab.

Horrified I asked, "Did the taxi sit here all this time?"

My aunt laughed. "I called while you were washing up."

I breathed a sigh of relief.

She told him the place and we arrived in about three minutes. We could have walked.

The neon sign near the roof had a man's grinning face sporting a large mustache. The giant word PIZZA flashed. Impressive. Music blared from the establishment as well as amazing smells causing my mouth water. I realized I hadn't eaten for a few days.

Auntie ushered me inside the warm atmosphere. A woman in slacks and shirt, wearing an apron, walked by. "Sit wherever you like."

Aunt Sherry led the way to a small table for two against the wall. The woman came over and handed us menus. "Have you been here before?"

"No. Can you suggest something?"

She grinned. "I'll get you the most popular pizza pie. Want a Coca-Cola while you wait?"

"Thank you, we both would." Aunt Sherry took care of everything. Did she know making a decision would be impossible for me?

A few minutes later, we got chilled glass bottles. I hadn't had one in a while. That first sip tantalized my tongue with bubbles and sweetness. Aunt Sherry set hers down. "Did you ever talk to that doctor?"

"Yes, a while ago. He told me all about that night. Did you know I died three times? Well, at least my heart stopped."

She nodded, waiting for me to go on.

"Twelve minutes."

"Twelve minutes what, sweetheart?"

"I died for twelve minutes and the other doctors wanted him to stop trying to make me live."

"That's a very long time. I wonder if that has happened before?"

I shrugged. "He had read about how to save someone's life that morning and he found me at the crash."

She reached across the table and took my hand. "Because he needed to save you. God has a purpose for you."

"Why? What could I possibly do for Him? Why would He pick me? I'm a nobody. Unimportant. Young. Alone."

Interruption

"Sweetie, you are not alone. You have me and the Lord. He is with you always. Tell me again how your momma greeted you and what she said."

I gazed over her shoulder and replayed it in my mind as I retold about my momma. The rest tumbled out. "Oh, Momma told me to tell you she would see you there someday."

Aunt Sherry smiled and peered into the distance.

She took a sip of her cola. "What you experienced is special, unique—a gift of extreme value. Don't ever forget it."

"That's just it, I had forgotten. A dream brought it all back. That's why I had to see Dr. Smith. Aunt Sherry, what if I forget?"

The woman came back and slid a large plate holding a round, flat-edged, crusted, gooey mass of melted cheese, in front of us. I caught glimpses of red sauce and meat, tucked under all the cheese and I guessed this to be pizza. It smelled wonderful and sizzled. She gave us two plates and a handful of napkins. "Enjoy."

Aunt Sherry scooped up a spatula full, landed a piece of the pizza pie on my plate, and then gave herself some. I lifted my fork and cut a bite. I blew on the steam rising and hoped I wouldn't burn my tongue. "Oh my goodness! Never in my life have I tasted anything so good."

Auntie laughed. "Honey, all your life, when you've tasted something new, you've expressed those sentiments."

Interruption

"Probably." I shrugged. But in my defense, I hadn't tasted anything like that gooey, cheesy bite. I knew I would forever remember this experience of eating my first pizza pie. Why were some things easy to remember but more important ones, easy to forget?

Chapter 5

Jacquelyn

On day two of our trip from Chicago to Grand Junction, I felt better, more rested. I slept away the last sixteen hours, having left mid-afternoon yesterday. Aunt Sherry, true to her word, let me do what I wanted and sleep took precedence. I vaguely remember the stops in cities and towns en route and only jarred awake a few times but slipped right back into dreamland.

I pulled back the curtains in the window and squinted at the bright day. Fields of perfectly straight rows of green grew out of dark earth. The sky was a powder blue with a few clouds, and the sun shone bright, though low, having recently broken the horizon. I decided to get up and dress. There must be more to this train than this small room. Hunger prodded me to venture out.

Interruption

I pulled on a pair of elastic waisted pants with a green pullover top and slipped into my canvas shoes. I finger-brushed my hair into a semblance-of-order ponytail.

The train clacked along the tracks and swayed slightly back and forth, so one needed to pay attention to keep balance. Maybe I experienced this sensation from being a bit weak from lack of food and water. Right or left? I peered at the number to our bedroom and went right. The progression of numbers suggested I headed in the correct direction.

I smelled the tantalizing aroma of fried breakfast meats, eggs, toast, and coffee. My stomach growled, demanding attention. The doors swooshed open and I walked into a room with tables and linens. Diners tinkled their silver against plates and lifted glasses or coffee cups to their lips. I peered down the long aisle with tables on each side and caught a glimpse of my aunt sitting with three men. I proceeded toward their table. Aunt Sherry waved. When I reached the table, the men stood as much as they could in the crowded space. "Jackie, these nice gentlemen are headed to Grand Junction as well. Let me introduce you, Mr. Peter Nichols, Mr. Eugene Wright and his son, Warren. And this is my niece, Jacquelyn Carter."

I shook their hands. "Please, call me Jackie."

Faphick

An amazing change came over Jackie when her aunt arrived at the institution. She pushed away Fear and Agitation and kicked Temptation and Dependency out of reach. I wanted to cheer. Sherry soothed and bolstered her and took Jackie to eat. The girl needed nourishment and human comfort and love. Sherry gave her all of that. If only my charge would turn to the One who loved her most.

People and spirits roamed the streets, restaurants, and the train depot. Busy Guardians protected their charges as Beings tried to trip up, discourage, belittle, and disrupt their confidence and faith. People went about their lives unaware of the danger of physical pain and emotional and mental distress.

On the train, Jackie rested well and fell into a deep sleep as I sang to her. The Lord on High informed me to let her sleep but stay vigilant. Her life sat firmly in His hands and He knew her future.

The Valiant Ones who guarded the men seated with Sherry were highly battle wary and trusted by the Lord on High. Impressed, I accepted the camaraderie and help. Very seldom did we get to enjoy each other's company during our missions.

Jacquelyn

The conversation at the breakfast meal went without a hitch. I had never enjoyed myself more in the company of virtual strangers. Aunt Sherry seemed to brighten even more than normal. The men were knowledgeable in all sorts of subjects. One or the other spoke of the sights we passed as well as their individual pursuits. Auntie held her own. I, on the other hand, had little to interject, but somehow I felt comfortable.

Auntie clasped my hand. "My dear niece is an accomplished dancer and has traveled all over the continental United States."

"Really? What kind? Ballet? Soft shoe?" Mr. Nichols leaned forward and rested his elbows on the now cleared table.

"Actually, tap." I smiled at the reaction from the gentlemen. Appreciation and respect.

"She not only traveled in a troupe but had leads in musicals that featured her lovely voice as well as her talented fast feet."

"Impressive. Give us a taste." Mr. Nichols smiled and nodded.

"Go on. We would love to hear you sing. The room's practically empty." Mr. Warren waved his hand.

Interruption

I turned and scanned the car. Only two tables had occupants far back on the other side. Still, I would feel foolish and I hadn't sung since my accident. What if I couldn't? What if my voice cracked or I sounded hoarse? I shook my head and pulled up my shoulders, wanting to shrink inside myself. "I don't think so."

"Come on, we will sing with you. How about a popular one everyone knows, 'You are My Sunshine'? You are my sunshine my only sunshine. You make me happy …" Aunt Sherry started and the men joined.

What else could I do? I slid in my soprano and halfway through the second verse they stopped and left me to carry the song to the end. "…Please don't take my sunshine away."

They clapped. I turned red. It felt good but embarrassing at the same time.

Auntie stood. "I'd like to walk a bit."

Mr. Nichols and Mr. Wright both rose and the latter asked, "I wouldn't mind a walk myself, may I join you?"

"I would love company."

"Peter, I'm sure the young set would enjoy time away from us old fogies. What ya say?"

"Can I interest you two in a game of Scrabble?"

"You're on." Mr. Wright led the procession and Warren and I were left alone.

"I hope my dad and Mr. Nichols didn't make you feel uncomfortable. If you want, I can take my leave."

"Don't be silly. Stay."

"I'm glad for a chance to get to know you. Would you like some ice cream?"

I giggled and nodded. "I will always go for ice cream even as a mid-morning snack." I followed him to the counter and ordered a cone. I got chocolate, and Warren, two scoops of strawberry.

The cold creamy delight and the crunch of the cone worked their magic. Soon good old-fashioned small talk led to a deeper discussion.

I answered his questions. "I trooped across the country with Mom until my fifteenth birthday. I figured I could take care of myself and sent her home to be with Aunt Sherry."

"How did that work for you?"

I ducked my head. Warren seemed a trustworthy sort but I didn't feel ready to talk about it to anyone, even myself. "We had so many shows I didn't have time to think about it. I missed her."

"Where is she now?"

A huge sadness engulfed me. "She died that year. I never saw her again."

"Oh, I'm so sorry. I didn't know." He clasped my hand. Concern drew his dark eyebrows together and his light blue eyes searched my face. "Do you mind me asking how she died?"

"Pancreatic cancer. She knew she had contracted it but kept it from me. She went fairly quickly. While she traveled with me, I didn't stop to think about her and why she seemed so tired and had pain." I couldn't do this. "Let's talk about something else. Your dad seems a nice guy. What about your mom?"

Warren removed his hand from mine, lifted his right leg, and rested his ankle on the knee of his left. "My mom is head nurse at Saint Mary's Hospital. Her schedule is full and so Dad decided to come alone to get me from the university in Chicago. I followed his footsteps in Psychology at his alma mater, where Mr. Nichols also attended. They hung out and went to sports events and attended lectures. We packed up my gear and boarded the train."

"What do you plan on doing with your degree?"

"Dad opened up his practice a few years ago. With medical training as a medic in the war and a psychology degree, one thing led to another. He went on staff at St. Mary's and after six years he jumped out on his own. Dad is one of those trailblazers and specializes in counseling psychology. The need for this is substantial since the war opened up this field."

"Are you planning on joining him in his practice?"

"That's the plan. Our office is near the hospital. What are your plans? Dancing?"

"I'm not sure. I lost my position with the troupe."

"Oh?"

Should I tell him? "I got in a car wreck and had medical issues. They couldn't wait and hired someone to fill my slot. From what I've read they are in Texas and playing for sold-out crowds."

"Do you miss it?"

"Yes. I miss the dancing but not the travel and sleeping in a strange place every couple of months. It got a bit lonely when Mom left." Why did I say that?

"I bet. I appreciate the fact I can work in practice with my dad. As soon as I have a good patient list, I'll find a place of my own to live. Right now, I live with my parents. It's good you have an aunt who seems real keen on you. Will you live with her?"

"For the time being, I suppose." I shrugged. "We haven't talked about it." I sat up and smiled. "She surprised me, waltzing into my room and whisking me away. She said, 'Get ready, I'm taking you to dinner.' We had pizza pie, which is delicious by the way. The next day we boarded this train."

"I'm glad you did, so I could meet you."

The heat rose in my cheeks. I felt the same.

Chapter 6

Jacquelyn

We had a stop-off in Denver and I remembered my childhood. All those years ago, Mom and I got off here and my career started in earnest. The bus line and the train used the same depot. The place held more people and none wore military uniforms like back in the forties but, other than that, it appeared the same. Passengers from our train were permitted twenty minutes to walk around and visit the gift shop.

I found a darling silver spoon engraved with "Denver" in the hollow and at the tip of the handle had a porcelain inset of a painted snow peak. Auntie sidled up to me and whispered, "I think that is adorable—a reminder of happy times here with your momma and this trip. Let's buy it." She always did spoil me. Not having kids of her own, she sort of latched on to me and had always treated me like her daughter. I appreciated her now, more than ever. With a quick stamping down of thoughts and emotions, I swallowed the knot in my throat and smiled up at her.

The paper sack held my treasure and we dashed back to the train. Giggling and out of breath, we collapsed on our chairs in our room. Sometimes, Auntie acted my age. Again, gratefulness heightened my appreciation for her.

"Come on, our traveling companions invited us to the observation car. They said they would hold seats for us." She clasped my hand and tugged me up.

Auntie led the way and we passed people in the crowded walkway. "Excuse me," I said and turned sideways each time.

True to their word, the fellas occupied chairs with two empty ones between them. Auntie sat between the older men and I sat between father and son. Overhead, glass gave us a great view of the sky and the sidewalls were windows as well. The mountains beckoned and the train wove across open fields before it started its ascent. A herd of antelope with their white behinds bounded away from the approaching iron monster.

Warren said, "I love this part of the trip. The tracks wind through amazing rugged places and the feat of the engineers to carve the tunnel and the beauty to meet us on the other side is incredible."

"What is it called?"

"Moffat. It opened in 1928 as a railroad and water tunnel to cut through the Continental Divide. Before that, the train had to overcome steep grades and snowdrifts that most often stopped the train."

Soon, the lower hills made way to a steeper climb. Blackness enveloped us as we went into the tunnel. Bright sunlight made me blink as we came out the other side. Again, there were towns where the train came to a stop to allow passengers on and off.

The impressive scenery of mountains, hills, trees, fields, towns, and small bodies of water paraded in front of me. This seat afforded delights of sightings of birds and animals as well as people. Sweeping by my lookout were small farms with tiny houses and a horse in the corral or cows in the field. An occasional truck or car on the parallel road sometimes traveled alongside, seeming to crawl along.

I was glad I got my sleeping over during the fields of Illinois and Nebraska so I could enjoy this marvelous sight before me. My companions pointed, drawing my attention to things I might miss. I appreciated this trip much more than I had at age ten on the bus and was grateful for the company of these charming and knowledgeable gentlemen. Auntie seemed to feel the same.

Hours into our trip, we stopped at Glenwood Springs. The train went past the famous hot springs. Mr. Wright said, "I heard they are doing an extensive remodel. In 1943, the navy commissioned a hospital and rehab here for injured soldiers. After they vacated, a small hospital continued but it all changed hands last year."

The train slowed and it pulled into the depot. Not wanting to lose our vantage point, we stayed in our chairs.

After the whistle, the train pulled away from the Glenwood Springs depot. About a half-hour out, we stopped at another town for people to come and go.

"Interesting way this town got its name." Mr. Nichols leaned closer so we could all hear. "A surveyor found a rifle in the dirt which seemed to have come from a trapper years before. Welcome to Rifle."

Warren nudged me with his elbow. "Would you like something to drink?"

I nudged him back. "Yeah."

We stood. "Auntie, would you like a cola?"

"I'd love one, honey."

"Colas all around, coming up." Warren placed his hand on my back and I led the way to the refreshment counter a few cars back, glad to stretch my legs.

I climbed up to sit on a high stool and leaned my elbows on the counter. Warren sat next to me. "Five Coca-Colas, please. Two now and three to go." The man turned and reached behind him and pulled out two cold bottles from the chest refrigeration unit. He popped the cap on a bottle opener mounted on the wall and placed them before us.

"Thanks." Warren counted out the change and slid it to the man.

I took a large sip. "Thank you. You had a great idea."

"You're welcome."

"How do you know so much about so many things? I mean, all three of you. I just take in the sights, but you bring another dimension to what I'm seeing."

Warren smiled. "Dad and Mr. Nichols challenge each other. I think they're enjoying sharing what they've learned to a new audience. Before my freshman year, we spread out a map of our trip and divided it up into parts. We each had four sections to research so we could share what we learned to the others. I'm afraid I didn't spend as much time at the library as they did. But I have been able to contribute." He took a long swig of his drink. "Those two bet each who could come up with the most impressive and obscure knowledge. Which, if challenged, the information has to be documented and checked. I didn't go that far and neither did Michael. The winner enjoyed a manicured lawn for an entire summer. Dad lost to Mr. Nichols and hired someone to fulfill the bet he lost."

"Michael?" I took another long drink.

"Oh, beg your pardon, Mr. Nichols's son. He stayed in Chicago. He got a terrific summer job that he hopes turns into a permanent position. I'll miss him. When we set off on our college years we promised we would come back home when finished. Some promises are meant to be broken or should never have been made."

"I'm sorry. Do you have other close friends?"

"He is my best friend. However, I have a few but so many of us have scattered. Do you have any childhood friends in Grand Junction?"

I shrugged. "I have no idea."

Faphick

A budding friendship. I smiled. Unlike Valiant Ones, people need friends. Jackie relaxed in his company. A new adventure and a different sort of person were both good for her. The teens she got involved with in the troupe had self-serving interests, and hurt her more than she had yet acknowledged. Time would tell how the damage would manifest itself. Many vied for her attention. Fear, Loneliness, Bitterness, Resentment, Blame, and Self-loathing fought to be heard and injure her. For the moment, she ignored them. I did what I had been commissioned to do but no more and no less. As soon as she rejected them, they were mine to dispatch.

Jacquelyn

The city sped by, shop upon shop, houses, and stores until the train slowed to a stop. Home. My home? Downtown, Grand Junction. I peered out the window at the depot and the scurry of uniformed men. Memories flooded my mind of when I last stood on a similar platform waiting with Mom for the bus to take us to Denver where I started my life as a professional dancer.

I remember being excited about the trip. I didn't know it would in all probability be my last time in this town. I didn't come back with my dear, sweet mother. I came back with Aunt Sherry who was really my rescuer. Did she know how much she had rescued me? What had the hospital and rehab people told her? How much of the last three years did she know? Mortification made me want to climb onto the pull-down bed and have it close me into the wall. Instead, I made sure I had everything I came with and followed Aunt Sherry through the tight hallway and out onto the platform.

Earlier, we had said our good-byes to the guys, promising to see each other again. I hoped so. Yes, I hoped so.

Interruption

Auntie hailed a cab. The cabbie lifted each of our bags and set them into the trunk and again, I slid in next to Aunt Sherry. She lived a bit outside of the city limits.

Sherry's husband, Uncle Bill, had been a successful banker. He'd purchased land and built them a lovely ranch house before he died. Nobody had been more astounded at the extent of his wealth, however, than his wife.

She hadn't known about it until the reading of the will. She said she almost fainted. Uncle Bill had kept his financial dealings to himself, telling her not to worry her pretty little head with all that nonsense. Mom, practical as ever, told her that she needn't let that change her and not to do anything but pray and grieve. God would tell her what her next step in life would be.

All these years, Auntie had lived quietly and kept on working as a receptionist at the dentist's office. Her letters had been long and full of love. She helped subsidize Mom and me while I danced my way across the country. Even after Mom left, I got a wire every time I landed in a new city. She kept up with me. What if she found out how I spent her money? She'd hate me.

I gazed out the window on the drive to her house and Auntie interrupted my musings. "Jackie, we don't have many outlets for professional entertainers here that can put more than a few bucks in your pocket. Have you considered school?"

I shrugged. I knew this would come up but I didn't want to think about it. "I don't know what to do. All I know is dance and music."

"I've given it a lot of thought. You should teach. Teaching is a reliable occupation. You could go into athletics, drama, or the music field—anything for that matter. Friday, we have an appointment at Mesa for you to take a tour and talk with the administration to enroll. You need to get on with your life and you are a talented person. I will pay for college and more counseling. This will be a private counselor who will help you with all life issues not just rehabilitation like you endured."

Oh my. I didn't see this coming. First things first. "I didn't graduate high school. I won't be accepted."

"I thought as much. I worked it out that you will be tested, given a GED. Mesa will accept it for your diploma and you can take college courses. Isn't this exciting?"

"Yeah, sure." I probably wouldn't pass. Then what? I know she means well. But. I turned and saw the sweet enduring smile. She had done so much for me all my life. I owed her. I smiled back and she patted my hand. I would do as she bid but I was afraid her money wouldn't be put to good use.

Faphick

As soon as Aunt Sherry started talking about Jackie's future, Self-doubt, Discouragement, and Self-loathing catapulted into the car with them. All the enthusiasm that had buoyed her up sizzled.

"Jackie, your aunt is trying to help. Please don't fight her. Don't listen to these vile Beings lying to you. You are not what they are saying. You are talented, brave, intelligent, and capable."

The Beings sneered and hissed their wicked words and she clasped them to her heart.

Chapter 7

1956
Jacquelyn

I teased the back of my hair to create height at my crown and smoothed it to the flip at the ends. A ton of hairspray and a bit of lipstick went next.

In the past before any performance, hairdressers and make-up artists transformed me into a persona for the stage. When the drugs and alcohol had taken over, those pampered times hadn't filled me with ease like they once did. I worried whether they would notice my addiction and nervous energy made me agitated instead of relaxed.

One last look in the mirror, a twirl in my party dress, and I felt ready for the arrival of the guests. I smiled at the girl I had become and felt grateful that awful time was gone. I still needed to somehow finish college, but Auntie kept reminding me "one day at a time." I scooted out and down the stairs, I didn't want to be late to my own party.

"Happy Birthday to you. Happy Birthday to you, Happy birthday, dear Jackie. Happy birthday to you." Auntie led the people in the crowded house to sing for me. I grinned and then blew out all nineteen candles.

There weren't any school chums. I trudged through my courses alone. Most of the people were Auntie's age but a few had brought their children and a few more were my age from church. Warren and some of his buddies showed up as well. All in all, a good crowd came to celebrate with me.

What a far cry from last year when I alone congratulated myself on another year alive. Auntie had sent her gift of a pretty pink scarf and a bit more in the account to pay my bills. But I sat in rehab and felt sorry for myself.

Today, smiles from new friends and Auntie filled me with warmth. Also in attendance was my counselor, a wizened older gentleman with soft intelligent brown eyes, who came highly recommended by Warren's dad. Sure enough, Auntie invited him and he readily accepted. Mr. Franks. I called him Prof Frankie. Had he come to scrutinize me away from our sessions? Did I need to watch what I said and how I acted?

"Jackie, everyone is asking. Why not give it a shot?" Auntie quietly pleaded.

I had heard the buzz of people asking me to perform. I wanted to, but what if I tripped? I hadn't danced in front of anyone in over a year. A month ago, I opened the box of my dancing costumes. There they were—my shoes. I put them on and did a small clappity-clap on the bathroom tile. Auntie had heard me and drove me crazy by prodding me to dance. I explained that my legs didn't want to cooperate the way they used to. Something had happened to afflict them during my accident.

Now, she tugged me to the living room where the bare floor waited, the rug having been rolled up against the wall. She thrust my shoes into my hands. I looked around at the expectant faces. Unable to refuse, I sat and slipped on my tap shoes, which fit like a glove—my old friends. I took a few experimental taps and some surreptitious stretches.

Auntie had the music going on the turntable before I stood up. A nice and fast tune I had danced to many times. I knew a whole routine for that number.

My feet remembered. Faster and faster, they went, until they messed up. I crashed headlong into the laps of older ladies sitting on the sofa. Embarrassed more than hurt, and expecting boos to chase me, I wanted to run into my bedroom. Instead, the room erupted in applause.

I peeked sideways through my hair that had covered my face. Smiles and encouragement met me. Amazed, I rolled to my feet and tucked my unruly hair behind my ears, and grinned. A little self-confidence came with it.

"I'm so sorry. Did I hurt you?" I bent to speak to the ladies that had moments before held me.

"Not a bit!"

"Wasn't that part of the routine?"

I giggled. All was forgiven. I didn't do so badly after all.

Faphick

I had orders to let Jackie trip. When she emerged triumphant, I cheered too, grateful for the All-Knowing One letting her fall.

During her tap dance, Cocky had stuck out the sword and tangled her feet as Regret and Self-Doubt pushed her. Her nemeses as of late, Regret and Self-Doubt, laughed at her dance and fall. Fear messed with her. I battled Reproach and Accusing.

The people broke into applause. Jackie stilled and shyly checked the faces in the room.

From the results of her fall, Cocky slipped back into the shadows.

Self-Confidence boosted people up and became the loudest voice. A foe had returned.

Each Being could only do what the Lord on High allowed and, at the moment, this one spoke inaudibly to her. Jackie stood a bit taller and her chin came up. She had danced well and would have continued had she been left alone.

Reproach, Accusing, Regret, and Self-Doubt backed off. For the moment, she only heard Self-Confidence. If she wasn't careful, Pride's talons would strike deep.

At that moment, prayers were lifted to the throne on her behalf. Aunt Sherry and a few of her close friends prayed for my charge and Pride slunk away.

Jacquelyn

Prof Frankie settled back into his chair. My regular scheduled appointments went like clockwork. Holding a cup of tea in my hand, I sat in an overstuffed blue corduroy chair waiting until he asked me how I felt.

"Jackie, how long have you been coming to see me?"

Not the question I expected. "Two months."

"Do you feel we are making progress?"

I shrugged. Where was he heading?

"Do you trust me?"

I snorted. "What? Is there something I shouldn't trust?"

"No. But you obviously do not. You sidestep my inquiries. If I'm to help you, you need to let me. Take down the wall. Let me see the real Jackie, the one you protect. Let me see into your relationship to your mom, your aunt, friends, those you worked for, and the ones at school."

I didn't like this direction of insistence and questions. Why the change? I had kept up my end of the bargain with Auntie—see Prof Frankie and go to school in exchange for a place to stay, and she paid for this and school. I thought it a sweet deal but now, not so much. I set my untasted tea down and stood. "Are we finished for today?"

Prof leaned over and pressed his intercom. "April, send her in."

I frowned. Who?

The door opened. Auntie breezed in. "Doctor Franks." She nodded and turned to me. "Jackie."

Oh, boy. I sighed.

"Mrs. Hartford, thank you for coming. Please have a seat."

Aunt Sherry snuggled into the other chair, all comfortable and relaxed. What were they up to? I looked from one to the other and waited.

Faphick

Jackie cringed when her aunt, who I knew had waited on the other side of the door, entered. The outward defiance of Jackie hid the timid child inside. Accusers circled, tossing their vile darts at her. Some I deflected, but others, she had accepted. Fear, Loneliness, Bitterness, Resentment,

Interruption

Anxiety, Self-Disdain, Uneasiness, and others vied to conquer. I didn't know which would win. I rooted for her and spoke truth to her but she only listened to the dark words pulling her down.

Three Valiant Ones stood against numerous Beings, each with an agenda. Only a few Beings were interested in the doctor and Sherry. Those two people had great faith and knew to Whom they belonged, and who they were, having already rejected those that now relentlessly badgered Jackie. The fierce battle waged.

Chapter 8

Jacquelyn

"Jackie, are you leaving? I thought the three of us could have a nice little chat." Aunt Sherry's brilliant smile showed no signs of guile. I shifted my gaze to Prof Frankie and couldn't read him. Good at his job, I never did.

Auntie had done so much for me and only asked two things. They seemed quite impossible and I had no way out unless I stamped out and left the comfort of her home, regular meals, friends I'd made, Warren, and her love. Those last two would kill me. I returned to my seat.

The clock behind me on the wall made its presence known. *Tick*, breath, *tick* breath, *tick*…

"So talk," I blurted. Oops!

Seemingly, unruffled Auntie said, "Jackie, are you happy here in Grand Junction?"

I shrugged. "I love your home and I like not being on the move all the time."

"I got a call from my friend Amy from Mesa University and it appears things are not going well with your studies."

I slid deeper into my chair. *Tick. Tick.* "I'm failing. I know! I can't help it! Everyone is so smart! I don't know anything. All I know is dance and I can't do that anymore. It's all I'm good at. All I learned all my life was rhythms and poise. Not much book learning. College is hateful! Nothing works for me. You expect too much!" I crumpled into a ball and wept bitter tears. I missed my momma.

Faphick

I knew this moment would come sometime. She couldn't hold it in forever. Relief for her and excitement for the healing to begin spread through me. The break had to happen first. The Beings paused, waiting. I cheered her on. "Let it out. Tell these people everything you feel. Spill your emotions." While I shielded her, I soothed with my voice. The Lord looked on. His kindness and love waited.

"Reach out, little one. Let the Lord on High touch you and comfort you. He is here waiting. Grab His hand."

Interruption

Jacquelyn

I felt Auntie's arms. "Oh, sweet Jackie, I had no idea. I thought your education had been adequate or I wouldn't push you to climb on board the education wheel. Honey, you passed the admission test. You have more learning than you realize. Are these the wrong courses? What do you want to do? Is there anything you ever thought would be fun to do?"

Did I dare? I sniffed. She handed me a tissue. I wiped the mess. She gave me another and I blew my nose. She took my soiled ones and handed me another, just like a mom. I felt a whisper to go ahead. I took a shaking breath. "You'll think it's a crazy idea."

"No, I won't. I promise. You can tell me anything. You've got my curiosity raised. Please tell me what you want to do."

"I want to be a clown." I waited.

"All right. We can work with that."

I peeked at her. "I'm kidding."

Tick. Tick. I threw my head back in laughter at her confusion. "You should see your face. I don't want to be a clown." I snorted. "I don't want to be in front of anyone ever again. It's not all fun and glamorous."

Interruption

I took a deep breath and sighed. "No." My body quaked. "To be examined and critiqued—to read your name in the paper in dismissive overtones—to be ridiculed by the audience and sabotaged by other dancers anytime you get praise." I shook my head. "You have no idea what it's like. I thought they were my friends. I...I...Oh, you don't understand." I fell apart. All the terrible stuff flooded my brain. I couldn't take it. The tears wouldn't stop.

Finally, there were no more. Tears had dried up. My tired eyes were dry, burning, and scratchy. A nineteen-year-old, crying like a five-year-old, wishing for her momma, yet at the same time grateful to have Auntie. I was pathetic.

She held me. "I know. It's all right. The alcohol and the drugs. I'm more interested in why and so, I want you to take me to where you were and what you were feeling."

Prof Frankie spoke for the first time. "Let's go back to when you got the cable about your mom."

I stiffened. No, not there. Momma. A lump formed, choking me. Momma. I missed her so much. Her face filled my mind's eye. Not the last time I saw her, but in Heaven— her beautiful, young, calm face. She had urged me to keep going.

"My world caved in. Even though she had been here living with you and not with me, I knew she rooted for me and seemed to be with me. Receiving word that she died devastated me. Not having her there for me anymore left a gaping hole. The support and comfort of her encouragement and love—gone forever. I couldn't bear it. I had already gotten involved with the wrong crowd. There seems to be a bad bunch in every group. When I made her leave, the loneliness almost killed me, but her death destroyed me. Lost, I drank even more and when the pain wouldn't leave, I took the pills they passed me. I figured, what did I have to lose?" My voice caught. Did I need to go on?

"Jackie, I'm terribly sorry I didn't fill your momma's shoes. I should've written more or called. Will you forgive me?"

Forgive her? What? I'm the one who needed forgiveness. I shook my head. "You didn't do anything but love me and provide for me. I'm sorry I used your money for drugs. I'm sorry I let you down."

"Oh, sweetheart, you are like my own flesh and blood. I think of you as the daughter I never had. You didn't let me down. The circumstances proved too tough for you. Wrong decisions were made. You've cleaned yourself up and are doing well. Do you know that I love you?" She lifted my chin.

I looked her in the eyes. "Yes."

"You didn't tell me what you really want to do. I get it that you don't want to pursue dancing professionally anymore. There must be something. Please trust me with your dreams."

Interruption

How could I explain?

Chapter 9

Faphick

I knew the bursting of the dam of pent-up emotions would bring debris to crawl over and trip her. I saw the joke for what it was—a diversionary tactic. She didn't want to tell her aunt. I kept whispering encouragement. The Lord called to her to trust Him and spoke to Sherry and to let her passion escape her lips. As a Valiant One, I didn't understand mortals and why they were so insecure in expressing themselves. Jackie had proved to be the same. There didn't appear to be anything wrong with what she wanted to do. The occupation had been successful for people and an upstanding one.

Pride of self for the accomplishment they did, and to stand up for oneself, was needed at times. When Pride took over, then it became a menace and could destroy. Always a fine line, I nudged Pride to speak louder. Jackie needed a prodding of Pride, Self-Acceptance, and Assurance. They bolstered her. I nodded. The Good Father approved when those Beings brought His children closer to realize who they were in Him and to a tighter relationship with Him.

Jacquelyn

I eased myself out of her embrace and sat straight in the chair. "Remember when I was a little girl, you let me fix your hair? Momma relaxed me by brushing mine. Some of my favorite memories are going to the salon to have my hair trimmed and a new hairdo introduced. I loved the upsweeps that I needed to wear while dancing. Then those rolls I had that called for an elaborate hairdo excited me. I sat in the stylist's chair and she fixed my hair. Those times, I felt like a princess. Pampered and adorned with braids and jewels in my hair. I want to do that for others. I want to make people feel special for a moment in time. A beauty shop where people leave their worries and cares outside the door and feel special, spoiled, coddled, and regaled. That is where I want to work. I want to become a—"

"Beautician." Auntie smiled at me as she finished my sentence. She didn't appear disappointed.

"You don't mind if I don't become a teacher? My heart is not into teaching children music, dance, or anything. I want to create beauty and dispense peaceful moments." My teeth clasped my bottom lip and I waited.

Tick.

"This is a wonderful idea! I can picture you standing behind a woman, both of you in the mirror. You explaining what you will do or listening to what she wants done. It's simply marvelous with your creative side coming out in helping women and giving them not only a moment of pampering but giving them confidence in their appearance."

"You understand." I let out a long breath. "I'm so relieved."

"We will go right now to the admin department at Mesa and withdraw your name and register you in beauty school."

"Before you go," Prof said, "I want to say, this is a good beginning but we need to dig deeper. Don't be late to your next appointment. Jackie, although I appreciate your aunt's help today, I expect you to continue to open up so we can help you not only get a hold on an occupation but to heal from wounds you have inflicted upon yourself and allowed others to harm you. Are we all in agreement?"

I had forgotten he sat in his chair, listening, and now had probes in his arsenal. I couldn't help the sigh. "All right. I agree and I'll be on time."

Auntie stood and swept her hand along her skirt to push out any imagined wrinkles. "If her classes intersect with her scheduled appointments we will change her appointment time. Thank you, Doctor Franks." She stuck out her hand and he stood to clasp it.

"Thank you for coming."

I didn't offer my hand. That had always been my silent rebuff and rebellion against coming.

Jacquelyn

The beauty school accepted me and I skated through the classes with enthusiasm. There I found camaraderie I'd never experienced. Girls of like-mindedness studied, laughed, and giggled. We took turns creating amazing hair designs on each other and volunteers. Sometimes they flopped and our teachers showed us how to redeem the mess before it turned into a disaster. The amazing part—I didn't have to change my appointments with Prof Frankie. The small school stood a short ten-minute bus ride to his office.

My mode of transportation came to a smooth stop and a hiss as the brakes settled in. The skinny old man bus driver pulled the lever. *Swoosh!* The door opened and, en masse, we stood to take our turn down the aisle and the three steps to the curb. A bit of independence for me to decline Auntie's offer to drop me off and pick me up. I told her, "I like the crush of people and the sights and sounds. I may never own a car. Who knows?" It was not like I had to lug a lot of books. A brush and comb was all.

I smiled at the driver, who nodded back, and walked four blocks to my appointment with Prof Frankie. My canvas shoes and slacks were comfortable for the trek on sidewalks past shops and stores. Aromas of burgers and fries radiated from the diner and music blared from the jukebox as I passed. A bakery with sugary delights tempted me as I passed the display in the window. Always up for a taste, I peeked in. Darlene smiled and motioned. "You're going to love this fudge frosting I made. Here, let me get you a taste." She handed me a spoonful. The creamy chocolate awakened my taste buds. My tongue swirled it around my mouth as I savored it until I swallowed. "That is amazing! Probably the best I've ever had. You are a wizard with the ingredients." Her generous lips parted into a contagious smile as she beamed at me. "Thank you. I'm so glad you like it."

"I'll owe you a free hairdo as soon as I finish learning how. See you next time." I headed down another block. A handbill on a light pole caught my attention about a sporting event at the local high school. I loved attending those. Warren, some friends, and I had gotten together and caught a few. Baseball, basketball, football, wrestling, and even track and field events interested me. I watched an occasional boxing match on Aunt Sherry's television.

Interruption

Anything sports and I was all in. I took note to tell Warren. I arrived at my appointment and opened the door.

April greeted me with a cup of tea and a smile. April always seemed glad to see me and made me feel welcomed and treated me as a friend. Not sure what Prof Frankie thought of me. April opened the door and I stepped into the intimidating room lined with books, the titles of which I could barely pronounce. The thick carpet and comfortable chairs did nothing to alleviate my trepid soul. How long would I be able to keep him at bay and not let him see the pain, I didn't know. This boxing match with feints and fancy footwork wore me out. How I managed to come out unscathed for the past months was an impressive miracle. Or was it? Maybe I should give up and rip it all open and spill my guts across his lap. *Did I trust him?* I wasn't sure what everything was deep inside of me. Did anyone really know themselves? What could come if I lost my grip. Those things were too dark to let loose.

Instead, I placed my bag on the floor and poured myself into the cozy, overstuffed wingback chair, acting casual but aware and primed for an uppercut or his right hook. I knew he would use muscle at some point. When? I had to be ready.

"Good afternoon, Jackie. How is beauty school? Remind me again of your new friends." Prof Frankie peered at me with a gentle smile and his brown puppy eyes.

Interruption

They didn't fool me. A killer lurked behind those pince-nez.

I sipped my tea, making him wait.

Tick. Tick. Tick. "I'm enjoying my classes. We're learning about the chemicals involved in delivering permanent curls to clients." I eyed him over the rim of the china cup. "They could be deadly you know, if someone were to ingest the proper amount." As I expected, he showed no outward reaction to my outlandish comment.

"As far as my friends go, they're the cat's meow. We get along well. A couple of us went bowling the other night."

"What did you score?"

"A perfect 150—half of a perfect game. Do you bowl, Prof Frankie?"

"I've done so. I take my family, on occasion, for an afternoon. Quite fun, really."

"So, little Frankies." I smiled at the picture that popped into my head. "I didn't know you had kids. How many and how old are they?"

"A boy, age twelve, girl age nine, and another girl age seven."

Unbelievable. Frankie was talking about himself. Why? "Three. Are you planning on more? How long you've been married?"

"Mrs. Franks and I have been married for seventeen years. No plans. We wait on the Lord. Did Warren go bowling with you?"

He used a feint. "Yes. A whole gang of us went and we had three lanes. Ate pizza and drank colas."

"Nothing stronger?"

Here it comes. "Now, Prof, you know I don't do that sort of thing anymore."

"Did anyone else in the group?"

He had me there. He probably had snoopy people who would tell. "A few of the older fellas did but most of us are underage." I gave him my most charming smile. "You don't have to worry about me."

"Did the smell bother you?"

"No."

"Entice you for a small sip?"

I shook my head. Where was this headed?

"Be honest. Didn't you for one moment want a drink? All that beer floating around the room in ice-cold mugs with foamy tops didn't call to you?"

Yeah, I could taste it now.

Tick. Tick. I licked my lips and took another long drink of the hot-spiced tea, bracing myself. "Yes. I still have temptation. Yes, sitting by a bottle or mug of alcohol is hard for me not to cave."

"Do you think you will ever get over that temptation?"

Interruption

I hung my head. "I thought so even though they said I wouldn't."

"Jackie, that is a fight you will have the rest of your life. Either you keep yourself far from it or you put on your armor before you go. You knew alcohol would be there. Did you go prepared?"

I set my cup on the end table beside me. "No. But I didn't have any so you need not go on about it."

"Because Warren came with you? Are you using him as a crutch?"

Again, he socked me. "I like Warren. We have fun together."

"Did you ask him to go with you because you needed him?"

"I like him. I want him there wherever we go."

"Have you told him about your life during drugs and alcohol?"

I didn't see that jab coming. I looked at the carpet. "Not all of it."

"Don't you think it's time?"

I nodded. Right again. Prof Frankie got those shots in before I could block them. They hit me between the eyes.

"Tell me about your friends when you were a kid."

I stared at him. This jab jarred my head back.

Tick. Tick. "I didn't have any except Mom."

"Did you play games? Go bowling? Swing in the park?"

My eyes stung.

Interruption

"Did she take you to roller-skating? Did you two build a fort? Climb a tree? Skip a rock in a lake?"

That did it. Tears traced down my cheeks. He got up and handed me another tissue.

Chapter 10

Jacquelyn

He let me cry for a moment as the clock indicated the seconds. I knew in my gut he wasn't finished with me today.

"Tell me why you're crying. How do you feel about not having a childhood?"

Tick. Tick. Tick. "I'm angry! I have never done those things! I didn't play with other children. We rehearsed. We competed. Why did I have to be the best? Work so hard? For what? She went off and died! She left me all alone with no one. No friends. All alone." My knees were up and I hugged them, sobbing hot angry tears.

"Didn't you send her away?"

"Yes! Yes, I did. Why did she do it? Why didn't she tell me no? I ne…never…sssaw her agaaain."

All of a sudden, arms held me. I peeked up. April. I leaned into her. Grateful for her caring about me and not letting me cry alone.

After I had control, she silently got up and left.

"Jackie, are you angry with your mom or yourself?"

I looked at him. I gave him my best frown. "Both. You already know that."

"Yes. And now you do, too. Now we can face your anger and work to heal. Are you ready?"

I shrugged. "Probably not. Who likes pain?"

"I don't know anyone who does. You are strong and the hurt will help you. The process of pain cleanses and begins the healing. Jackie, you didn't know you weren't ready to be alone. You didn't know your mom had cancer and you wouldn't see her again. You can forgive yourself for that. Your mom thought she did the best thing by leaving you. She knew she couldn't take care of you as she wanted while dying of cancer. She also knew you couldn't stop cancer and you were on tour. She did what she thought best in the situation. You can forgive her.

"Your mom watched your dad die before doing what he wanted to do with his life. She wanted you to do something special and sensational. You accomplished that. You broke out of the family mold of working in the mines or cleaning and sewing for others. Your mom made sure you used the talent the Good Lord gave you. I saw a glimpse of your talent at your birthday party. I can imagine how impressive you were on stage. You can forgive her for being a protective and farsighted mother. Hard work got you where you were, but, Jackie, how did it all end?"

That sucker punch knocked the air out of me. So smoothly, he turned the conversation on me.

Tick. Tick. Tick. Tick. "I threw it away in drugs and booze. I recklessly tossed away my career." I bet he didn't expect me to spill it so easily.

"Yes, you did. Good job to own it." He nodded. "You messed up. Have you asked the Lord to forgive you?"

Darn him! That hit below the belt!

Faphick

In the room where Jackie had her session with the doctor, chaos ravaged. Beings warred over her. She battled with them and herself. The doctor poked and prodded her in the right direction. Jackie likened their duel to a boxing match. I had been to many of those in my life. Some were a fair fight but others were not. In this one, although she felt the questions as blows, fairness came at every turn from the professor. As a doctor cuts out the infection to save a life, this man used his words to garner a reaction so her troubles and harbored resentments could ooze out.

Pride swelled in both her and the professor because of her admission. When she broke down and needed comfort, I called upon April's Guardian to help—who appeared to Jackie as April. Unseen by Dr. Franks, the Guardian came and comforted my girl, who thought the comfort came from April. Guardians and other angels can take on human form or can appear only to one person like April's Guardian did this time. The Lord on High told His people in His Word of this happening.

Jackie needed consoling. And as such, she opened up more and more. The best question needed asking and he did it at the perfect time. Would she ask the Lord to forgive her? We all waited for her answer.

Jacquelyn

I left the session with homework. I needed to talk to the Lord but I had never really learned how. Prof Frankie said I should talk to Him as my father. I reminded him I was unschooled in that concept. He said to speak to Him as I did Warren or Warren's dad. Only trust Him more and be open and honest.

That would be difficult.

Interruption

I ate my dinner of fried chicken and mashed potatoes with peas on the side, not tasting a thing. While Auntie droned on about looking for plants at the nursery and grocery shopping, I worried over what to say to God.

Finally, I excused myself and went to my room to get it over.

I changed into my pjs and knelt by my bed like I once saw someone do in a movie. "Lord, ah, Father, I got caught up with some people I shouldn't have. Had Mom been...sorry. It wasn't her fault. My fault. I made the choice to hang out with the wrong crowd. I took the pills offered to me. I drank beer and then harder liquor. I took more and more pills. You see, I missed Mom. Momma." My voice caught and I swallowed the lump. "I guess I blamed You for that, too. I'm sorry I sinned and ruined my career and almost my life. I never did thank You for saving my life. Also, Heaven is glorious. Thank You for taking me there. I loved seeing the beauty and my family. Especially Momma. Was it Jesus who took me around and hugged me? It must have been Him, so kind and handsome and easy to talk to. Help me not to forget it all. Jesus said He had a plan for me, something special. Can You give me a hint? I don't want to miss it or mess it up. Well, that's all I have to say now. Good night. Oh. Sorry. Someone told me once to end my prayer, 'in Jesus' name, Amen.'"

I felt better but something still bothered me.

Interruption

Momma.

A weight like a boulder slammed into my chest. I couldn't breathe.

Momma.

The lump in my throat grew. Tears stung my eyes. I buried my head in my arms on the bed and sobbed. "I tossed her out! It's my fault! I never saw her again. Why did I do that? Why didn't she stay? Why didn't You stop me from pushing her away? Lord? Why?"

Tears drenched my sleeve. I don't know how long I cried. Then I remembered what Prof Frankie said. I could forgive her, God, and myself.

"Lord, I'm trying. She looked so happy and beautiful in Heaven. She is better off there. I miss her terribly. It wasn't her fault. As Frankie said, I didn't know she would die. She only wanted the best for me. Father, help me to forgive her and myself. Help me to forgive You. Do You really know everything? You knew this would happen? You allowed it? I hope someday You will let me in on Your reasons. But, as Jesus said, I need to trust Him, You, and the Holy Spirit. Wow! All three of You together working on my behalf. Groovy! Thank You! Father in Heaven, I forgive You. Will You please forgive me?"

He did and I felt it. Amazing. A huge weight lifted off my shoulders. The tears stopped. Peace flooded me as if I'd plunged into a calm, clear, warm sea that refreshed me. I got up feeling tremendous—the weight of guilt lifted. I turned out my light and crawled into bed. I curled up and thought about the most beautiful place—Heaven.

Faphick

As soon as Jackie started to pray, the Beings melted away from her. Each tear of her repentant heart sent them scurrying. I enjoyed popping each one with the flat side of my sword as they left.

Anger, Blame, and Bitterness went most reluctantly with choice words, promising they would return. I hoped and prayed she wouldn't allow them back. Fear stayed in the shadows. Her unknown future frightened her. Would she banish Fear as easily? Unrecognized by Jackie, Fear held on and whispered doubts.

Although she enjoyed her beauty classes and did well, she still harbored Fear for her future. Thoughts of where she would set up shop or join an already existing operation had her all in jitters. She rarely acknowledged Worry although Worry and Fear played games with her emotions like the game of ping-pong that Jackie and Warren played in his garage at his folks' house.

Interruption

I stepped in when orders allowed and remained watchful on Jackie's behalf, all the while attentively listening to Almighty God.

Chapter 11

1957
Jacquelyn

The beautician school held a small ceremony for our class of twenty-five. I proudly walked up when they called my name. This made it possible for me to start my new career and my excitement mounted.

At the end of the ordeal, Auntie hugged me and examined my graduation certificate. "I am so very proud of you. You worked hard and have found your second passion. I have something to show you on the way to your party." She grabbed my hand and pulled me to her car. Over her shoulder, she called, "Warren, come on!"

I heard his steps as he approached, grabbed my certificate, and clasped my now free hand. As we rushed along with Auntie, he kissed my cheek. I giggled. He whispered, "I'm proud of you too."

"Thank you." I gave him a fleeting grin.

"Mrs. Hartford, what's the rush?" Warren called to my aunt who raced a few steps ahead.

"You'll see. And…" She winked. "We don't want to be late for Jackie's party." Auntie unlocked the passenger side and scooted around to unlock and get into her 1956 powder blue and white hardtop sedan.

I tossed my cap and gown into the back and slid into the front to sit in the middle. Auntie zoomed out of the parking lot, headed toward downtown Grand Junction, going the opposite way from her house where my party should be starting in less than a half hour. This party would be the second party I'd had in my life and I didn't want to be late. Seeing the excitement in Auntie's eyes made me accept that possibility.

Soon she pulled into a narrow parking spot on Main Street. She climbed out. "Hurry up, you two."

I shook my head as I scooted after Warren. He took my hand to help me gracefully place my three-inch heel-clad feet on the curb. Auntie never seemed to mind the awkward feel of heels. Graceful feminine steps glided her everywhere she went. She could probably run in them. I had only ever worn taps, flats, or sneakers until today.

Auntie trotted up to a door and put a key into the lock. "Jackie, Warren, enter." She swept her arm for us to go before her. She flipped on the lights. A black and white checkerboard floor gleamed. Hot pink salon chairs, three on each side, faced giant mirrors with small tables that held an assortment of hair implements.

Behind me, Auntie said, "Well, what do you think?"

"This place is amazing. Whose is it?"

"Yours."

"What?" I spun around and almost lost my balance but Warren caught me.

"Everything you need is right here. All you have to do is hire other beauty consultants and a manicurist." She frowned. "Maybe a receptionist? I don't know all the ins and outs. You're the owner and main stylist. First things first, pick out a name for this place. What do you want to call her?"

"I…I don't know what to say." I swallowed. My mouth had gone dry, probably from holding it open.

"Honey, this is incredible. Your aunt has handed you the world on a silver platter." He wrapped his arm around my upper arms and gave me a firm shake, jarring me to reality.

I stepped forward and took my sweet aunt into my arms. "Dear Aunt Sherry, this is too much to take in. I can't believe it. What about the job offer I accepted and start next Monday?"

"I called them." She cupped my cheek. "Don't worry about that. Tell me what you think? Are there enough chairs? At the other end, across from the hairdryers, there's a wash station." She pulled me down the slippery floor to two sinks and chairs. "You'll have to order products. I didn't know what you'd need. The other things came with the set-up. I picked fuchsia salon chairs because there're so bright and cheery." She turned and scurried across the spans. "Over here…" She pointed to the row of chairs and matching hooded hairdryers. "Is where people escape into the magazine world while the sound of the dryers cancels out noise. I added this rack for the magazines." Her manicured fingernail fanned through the titles on the wall rack.

She had thought of everything but I still didn't have words. I hugged her again. "You're too good to me. I don't deserve this." Then my mouth rattled on. "I don't know if I'm ready. I just finished school. Why would people rush to my shop?"

"Oh, that's just jitters. You'll do great." She hooked her arm with mine and led me back to the front waiting area. She sat and patted the spot next to her. I perched on the black Naugahyde bench.

"There'll be a learning curve, but you'll master that in no time. I can picture it all." She arced her palm in a slow semi-circle in front of her. I tried to see it through her eyes. It seemed pretty cloudy to me.

"We better get to the party. Jackie needs time to digest this wonderful news." Warren rescued me. He clasped my hands. I stood and he led me back to the car. My thoughts swirled like a tornado across the plains. She meant well. But I hadn't been consulted.

Faphick

I knew this would be hard for Jackie. Another well-meaning human did something for her that she had no control over. First of all, Jackie had become a child prodigy, on the road with her mom. Then her mom died. A terrible car accident that should have killed her came next. Her aunt moved her back to her hometown, sent her to school and counseling. Even though those things were for Jackie's good, she wasn't allowed to make any of the choices. The only choice she had made gave her Grief—sending her mom away. Not to mention all the Beings who leeched onto her, begging to take hold, and whispered outrageous words to take her down. No wonder her soul and spirit plummeted as soon as her aunt made her aware of her next phase in life. But You already know all of this, Lord God on High. You ordained and allowed these events.

I stood ready for action and waited. Warren understood Jackie better than Sherry did. He stepped in at the right time. Good for him. His Guardian nodded his approval, as did I. Their future appeared bright if I read the signs correctly.

Chapter 12

Jacquelyn

Auntie rushed us to the party. Grateful for Warren's warm reassuring hand holding mine, I tried to quiet my jumbled mind. A shop waited for a name and me. How would I manage? I didn't know one snippet of how to run anything. I hadn't ordered my life well and now she expected me to run a business? What in the world got into her thinking?

She pulled into the driveway. People milled on the front porch and the lawn. The front door stood open and I heard music coming from within. Someone had started the party. Warren squeezed my hand and got out. I followed and he helped me to my feet. "Jackie, smile, it'll work out. Enjoy your party."

I smiled at his handsome face. "Okay. You're right. I'll worry over everything later."

I followed Auntie into a full house. My old and new friends from school and church snacked on food and sipped drinks. Waiters carried trays to replenish the food stacked on the table in the dining room. I turned and took her hand. "Auntie, this is incredible. Thank you. You keep surprising me. I didn't expect anything so, so…"

"You're welcome. You deserve a big day. You worked hard and passed with flying colors. I wanted to mark this event for you and give you memories. You can do anything you put your mind to. You entered the classes late and caught up and aced them all. I'm proud of you so I wanted to give you this party and the shop as a graduation gift. You're the daughter I never had. Your momma, I'm sure, is smiling down from Heaven, beaming at her all-grown-up baby."

My eyes clouded. I rapidly blinked and willed the moisture not to fall. I hugged Auntie. "Thank you."

Jacquelyn

I cut the ribbon on *Curl Up and Dye,* with fifty or so people in attendance. A few weeks before, I hired two beauticians and a manicurist. Each had a small following, so we had appointments booked. Start small and build slow and steady could be my motto. Regardless of Auntie's enthusiasm, I put my foot down to do just that.

I consented to let Auntie cater the event. Pink punch, chocolate cake with white frosting, veggies, and potato chips sat on a low table for guests to enjoy. A fishbowl held pieces of paper with printed names to draw for one free haircut and style. To get their name included in the drawing, they had to set up an appointment. At the moment, October had appointments scattered throughout to keep us all busy, leaving slots for walk-ins. I hoped they wouldn't cancel later. Risk was what it was.

Warren had been a rock to lean on and an encourager to buoy my spirits. He lifted a paper cup. "Congratulations to Jackie and *Curl Up and Dye* for a successful opening."

"Hear, hear," came from a chorus of potential patrons.

"Aunt Sherry, will you please do the honors of drawing the name of one lucky person?" I lifted the clear bowl.

Sherry reached in and swished around and around, dragging out the anticipation. She lifted a piece of paper. "Theresa Thompson."

Theresa shrieked and ran to me.

"Congratulations. I'll tape this to your scheduled appointment," I found her name in the book and attached the slip. "A week from Thursday at two in the afternoon with Ellen." On a business/appointment card, I wrote her name and the word free and handed it to her. She waved it in the air as she hurried back to her friends.

Her excitement snagged at my heart. "Auntie, could you draw another name please?"

Auntie raised her eyebrows and then grinned. She winked at me as she plopped her hand in the bowl and swirled it around. "P.J. Sear."

A less ecstatic customer came forward. I found her name and added the paper. "Okay P.J., Friday at ten in the morning with me." I filled in another card and handed it to her. I smiled. "See you then."

Warren walked over and whispered, "A brilliant move. You showed that people are more important than the dollar. You've talked about caring and doing for others, you demonstrated that for two women you didn't know two hours ago. I'm proud of you."

"You know what could really make this place take off?"

He frowned and shook his head.

"Be my first patron. Let me cut your hair."

His eyes grew large. "I thought this place held a women's only club status?"

"Well." I shrugged.

"How about drawing another name but stipulate they get it done now?"

I laughed. "Brilliant!"

I turned to get everyone's attention. "Excuse me!"

A hush descended. "I would like to draw another name but this time, the participant has her hair done right now, during the party. What do you all say?"

Silence.

"Raise your hand if you are willing to get a free wash, cut, and style right now?"

Hands shot up. I let out my breath. "Warren, would you pull out a name, please?"

Warren set his cup down and reached in and pulled out a slip. "Tiffany Burgess."

Tiffany, hugely pregnant, stepped forward.

I asked, "Is right now doable for you?"

She grinned. "My last hurrah, I suppose."

"Well then, follow me." I said with more confidence than I felt. Why had I gotten myself into this? My first appointment to be carried out in front of everyone. What if my scissors slip and I cut a chunk off her hair? Or worse, cut her skin? I felt myself quake. "Please have a seat." I shook out the cape and clipped it in place. What if she goes into labor? I met her eyes in the mirror. She smiled and settled back. I took a deep breath and slowly let it out. I'd had months of training. A form filled the mirror. I looked up into Warren's confident smile. He gave me a nod and sat in the chair behind me. I said, "Are you next, Mr. Wright?"

"I just like the view."

I met his eyes. That was a mistake. My stomach flipped and I felt the warmth spread up my neck and into my cheeks.

Jacquelyn

"Jackie, how has the first week treated you? Good party, by the way. My wife said she booked appointments for herself and the girls." Prof Franks leaned back into his chair.

"Yes. I believe they're booked for next Tuesday. It's been a whirlwind of activity. I'm trying to do without hiring a receptionist. Although, dropping a curl to go answer the phone isn't a good idea. Auntie came in to lend a hand on her day off, which helped. I don't know what to do."

"Would having another person there help you make more money?"

"Eventually, it might."

"What are you afraid of?"

I bit my lip. I had begun to feel more comfortable spilling my troubles all over his office but did I dare this time? Would he let it slide?

The beastly clock ticked the time as I wrestled. *Tick. Tick.* Grr. "So far, I've not done life well. What if I fail and I can't pay Auntie back?"

He took off his glasses and rubbed them with his hankie. "Do you have a loan with your aunt?"

I shook my head. "Not per se."

Interruption

He slipped the glasses on. *Tick. Tick.* Oh. Now he waited. Trying to make me squirm? I wouldn't give him the satisfaction. I crossed my legs and took a sip of my Earl Grey tea.

"What did you give your aunt for Christmas?"

What? I thought I'd hit a homerun with my confession but instead, he snagged the ball. "I bought her a nice sweater."

"How did you come upon money for the gift?"

"I took babysitting positions in my spare time."

"Did you get the jobs specifically for her gift?"

"Yes, and I bought Warren a book he had mentioned. Why are you asking about Christmas?"

"Did you expect them to give you a gift in exchange?"

I scrunched up my cheek. "No. I gave them gifts because I love Auntie, and Warren is my friend." That was a base hit if I ever saw one.

"Did you give them a bill for the cost of the gift?"

"That's crazy talk."

"Of course it is. Your Aunt Sherry, out of love for you, purchased the shop and filled it with lovely things so you can do what you're passionate about and to have a way to make a living. And to put the cherry on top, you are your own boss. Make it work or not, doesn't matter to your benefactor." He tiled his head. "Would you take the sweater back if Sherry never wore it or take back the book if Warren didn't read it?"

"No."

"If you fail, will your aunt stop loving you?"

"I guess not."

Tick. Tick. Tick. Tick.

"No. She would still love me." Of course, I knew this deep in my soul.

He nodded. "Yes, because she did it—for you. It could've cost triple and she would have wanted to gift you the shop. Gift it to you. A gift is not a gift if there are strings attached."

Tick. Tick. Tick. "I don't know what to say."

"Did you tell her 'thank you'?"

I nodded.

"Even though you didn't get a say in the process?"

Whoa. He triple-played me. Not safe, like I thought, as I slid into home plate. Out! I hung my head. How had he known?

Faphick

Emotions and Beings sailed all over and bombarded Jackie. Admiration for the Professor rose in me. He listened to the Holy Spirit to know how to shoot the arrows into the real problems by asking the hard and direct questions. His Guardian's sword flashed around, as did mine. We conquered some Beings but left alone the ones permitted to be there.

For a while now, Jackie had been experiencing emotions from elation to fright. Daily she listened to Doubt, Self-Degradation, Fear, and Inadequacy. Pride reared up and demanded she should have been consulted on the matter.

For weeks, the battle raged. Fiery darts with uncanny accuracy sailed to penetrate her willpower. I comforted as much as possible but she had the final say. I spoke truth and sang to her. I protected and soothed her as she slept. Disrupted sleep gave Anxiety a stronghold. Her dreams reflected the turmoil inside. Tossing and turning. Moaning and shudders quaked her sleeping form.

At this moment, she needed to understand and let go. She had come so far but still had a way to go. "Jackie, talk it out. Tell the Professor what you feel. Let him help you process." I echoed the Holy Spirit. Would she hear us and take the sage advice? I peered toward Heaven. God on High watched and His love reached and swirled around her. The Holy Spirit, Jesus, and the Father drew her and waited patiently for her to make a decision and trust Them. The harmonic Trio loved her completely. "Please, Jackie. The Father loves you. He is using the Professor to help you. Give in. Let go. Kick the Beings away. Resist the Evil One and those who do his bidding."

Interruption

Jacquelyn

Time stood still.

No. The clock spoke, *Tick.* I didn't know how to answer Prof Frankie. *Tick.* The voice in my head yelled it wasn't fair. I should've been asked! I should've been asked. I. "I should have been asked! She didn't ask me! She just did it all. I would've been perfectly fine working for someone. How dare she do it all behind my back! Why didn't Momma tell me she was dying? Why didn't I ever get a say? When I did get a say, it ruined my life!" Oh! My voice betrayed me. I buried my face in my arm resting on the armrest.

Chapter 13

Jacquelyn

"Jackie. Here, sit up and drink this."

I vaguely heard Prof Frankie's voice.

"Jackie. Have some water. It's all right. Everything will be fine."

I pulled myself upright and I took the glass of water. My hands shook. Water sloshed out. His hands wrapped around mine to steady the glass to my lips. I drank. He took the glass. "Feel better?"

I nodded. I couldn't feel worse. Could I? Yes, a minute ago I had. Overreaction? Yeah. Big time. Why did I always do that here?

"It's all right to be hurt when you weren't consulted about the shop. But gifts are given out of love, and the recipient, most times, has no say in the matter. The best gifts ever given are not chosen by the recipients. No one would have considered the gift—too costly or extravagant or unique. God the Father sent His Son, Jesus Christ, to come to Earth to be born by a miracle—a virgin. Jesus Christ, the second in the Godhead, reduced Himself to take on human form so He could live and experience humanity. This way, He could empathize with our problems and became the example for us to follow. He obeyed His Father and yielded up His body to die on the cross most brutally, shedding His blood to pay the price of sin caused by humankind. A perfect sacrifice had to be made and He alone qualified. God the Father gave the gift of His only Son. Jesus Christ gave the ultimate gift of Himself for you. For me. For all mankind.

"We didn't ask for this gift. We wouldn't have known to think it up. The gift came without strings attached. It came out of the overflowing of Love. Have you accepted this amazing free gift of salvation?"

He made it so clear. "Yes. I remember, at the age of seven, I accepted Christ as my Savior. He paid for my sin." Another tear slipped down my cheek. This time, I didn't mind.

"He chose you and loves you. He has been there with you through everything, every moment in your life—the good times and the bad times. He didn't ask you to pay Him back. He keeps giving. He gives grace freely. He gives of Himself to you. He walks with you. In fact, He is here, right now. He calls you to trust Him in this situation and in every situation you go through."

He got up and walked back to his chair.

"He told me."

Prof Frankie frowned. "He told you?"

I stared across the room and brought the images up. "Yes. In Heaven. He said to trust them, the Father, the Holy Spirit, and Himself. Jesus is beautiful. All of Heaven is gloriously beautiful. I have to remember. I can't let it fade away. I keep trying to do everything on my own. You're right, He wants me to trust Him." I retold my story of dying and going to Heaven.

I brought my eyes to Prof Frankie. "Jesus said I had a job to do. What do you suppose He meant?"

Chapter 14

Faphick

I cheered. The other Guardian cheered. The Beings cringed. The pictures Jackie saw came from God on High. He flooded her memory with the heavenly world she had visited. She wanted to see, so He helped her remember. Light from the Trinity swirled throughout the room. The choir in Heaven lifted their voices in praise. I lowered my weapon and knelt in His presence. Too beautiful for mortals to behold, He warmed the room, and His never-ending love radiated and vibrated like a pulse of a human heart. Silence from the Beings contrasted with the melodic uproar in Heaven. The words and notes were precisely spoken by the choir and the Living Creatures around the Throne—all for the glory of God on High.

The people and Beings felt the presence of the Lord fill the room. The unwanted Ones scampered away.

The weight of Doubt and Fear lifted. Jackie pushed them away. Confidence and Peace flooded her emotions. Calm settled over her.

I hoped this lasted. I prayed she'd let the Lord's peace and comfort that resided in her fill every nook and cranny in her mind, will, and emotions. That she would allow the Holy Spirit to guide and comfort her.

"Good job, Jackie! Hang on to the Lord. Let Him lead you. Trust Him with everything. See how wonderful it feels to get yourself out of the way and kick the bad influences out of your life and have Him completely fill you?"

A chorus of praise from the other Guardian and myself lifted to God on High. Jackie's and the Professor's hearts sang out and joined us in adulation. These moments were the closest we came to unity with mankind.

Jacquelyn

Prof Frankie leaned forward. "Jackie, I can't answer that. Have you asked Him about your purpose? Have you prayed for Him to reveal an answer?"

I shook my head. "Will He answer me? Does He answer out loud?"

He sat back. "Jackie, God answers, but how He answers is unique for the individual He is speaking to. You may hear Him through a knowing in your soul, through His Word—the Bible, or through things others say. He can speak to you in a dream or in a song you sing while praising Him. You could be communing with Him outside in His beauty and hear His small, still voice as Elijah did. He knows you intimately and understands how best you receive His voice."

"Wow. I didn't know that." I shook my head. Imagine. God had a personal way to speak to only me.

Prof Frankie nodded and formed a steeple with his hands. "Pray, praise, ask, and take opportunities to be quiet before Him. He used Sherry in your life. She has provided for you. She gifted you. The Lord probably prompted her to buy the shop for you. No, you weren't asked. Are you upset about that anymore?"

"No. You're right. She did it out of love for me. I need to be grateful and thank her."

I glanced at the clock whose voice didn't challenge. I stood. This time, I stuck out my hand. "Thank you, Professor Franks."

He clasped my hand. "Jackie, you can call me Frankie. It's grown on me."

"Ha! Ha!" He'd tossed a curveball. He was a good counselor. I must remember to thank Auntie and Warren for choosing him. I needed to thank people more often. "Thanks. See you next week."

"I look forward to it."

I opened the door and looked back before leaving. He wore a genuine smile. I grinned back and then went out and hugged April. "Your boss is all right."

I headed to the bus stop. The sky above held white, fluffy clouds stacked against the deep blue. Thunderheads. They would build up and pull moisture into them until the heavy rain came crashing down onto the earth. That must be like me. I had been overwhelmed with pent-up emotions. Tears had to erupt today. I've never cried so much. Now, for some reason, I wanted to dance to the bus and giggled to myself. What would people think if I tap-danced down the street? I peered at my feet. These rubber soles wouldn't do. Excited, my fluid movements took me to the bus and my seat. I couldn't wait to see Auntie and thank her.

At home, I ran up the driveway and into the house. Quiet. Strange. I should hear her activities in the kitchen preparing dinner. She must have it ready. I checked my watch. Only five minutes later than I typically arrived home.

I pushed open the swinging door to the kitchen. "Auntie, it smells wonderful! What's for…" She lay crumpled on the floor. I rushed over to check her. Breathing. But her skin felt clammy. "Oh, Lord! Please don't take her too! I can't bear that!"

Call for help.

I hurried to the wall phone and dialed zero.

114

Interruption

"Hello? Please, I need an ambulance. My aunt collapsed. Can you patch me through?"

I waited. "Oh, Lord! Hurry them up!"

Tears burned my eyes.

"Yes. I need an ambulance. It's my aunt. I found her on the floor. Breathing, but out cold and clammy."

"What is your address?"

"Twenty-four ninety-nine Claimjumper Canyon."

"Out by Redlands?"

"Yes. Out past Redlands, off route 340."

"We are on our way."

"Please hurry!"

Chapter 15

Jacquelyn

With shaking hands, I put the telephone receiver down, ran over, tore off my jacket, and rolled it under her head. "Auntie, can you hear me?"

No response.

I stumbled back to the phone and after a few tries, dialed Warren's number, grateful I could remember.

I heard his voice and felt better.

"Warren, I found Auntie on the floor. Unconscious. Can you come?"

"Oh, honey, did you call for an ambulance?"

"Yes. They're on their way."

"They will probably beat me there."

"But you might."

"I'll head out right now."

"Thank you!" I hung up, ran over to the front door, left it open for the medical people, and then ran back to Auntie. I picked up her limp hand and reached up to the counter for a towel to wipe the moisture off her face. "I called for an ambulance. They should be here in a while. Hang on. Warren will come too. He might not get here first but I hope they all arrive soon. What happened? Oh, Auntie, can you hear me? I want to tell you I love you and thank you for all you've done for me all of my life. I love the shop. Thank you for the gift. I didn't understand and I felt frightened. I don't want to blow it. I don't want to mess it all up. I... Oh, Aunt Sherry. Please wake up and be all right."

I curled up next to her on the floor and pulled her hand up to my cheek. My sweet, giving aunt. I couldn't bear it if she died too. "Oh, Lord God in Heaven, please let Sherry stay with me. I need her. I love her. She's all I have. I never realized how much I need and love her. You already have Momma."

I heard the siren. It grew louder as it neared. Soon the noise stopped, boots pounded up the steps, and into the house.

"Back here!"

Two men in white pushed into the kitchen.

I got out of their way.

They knelt next to Auntie. "What's her name?"

"Sherry Hartford. I'm her niece and closest relative. I live here with her. I found her when I came home."

The door swung open and Warren stormed in and caught me up in his strong arms. "Jackie, I'm here. I'm sorry. They'll look after her."

Jacquelyn

The hospital ward held four beds. Aunt Sherry occupied the second one on the left, with a white blanket pulled up to her chest and her arms resting next to her torso. I approached and saw she appeared better with more color. The room buzzed with lowered voices from visitors to other patients.

I stood at her feet, marveling she lived. Yesterday, fright had taken hold. I didn't have enough faith. I worried they were wrong and she would be taken away from me. She opened her eyes, locked them on mine, and smiled. I hurried over and clasped her cool fingers. I hooked my foot around the leg of the metal chair and tugged it over so I could sit to be even with her. "You look good. Auntie, you worried me."

"Oh. You shouldn't let a silly thing like that worry you."

"Silly? You were out cold on the floor. I hadn't realized you were sick and found you, not knowing how long you had been on the floor."

Interruption

"I'm sorry I frightened you. I didn't know I had gotten so sick. I thought I had a tiny bug." A slight shrug of her shoulders and she continued, "Nothing to worry about."

"The doctor told me you have pneumonia and are dehydrated. It could be serious. They want to watch you and might put you on oxygen. You need to take better care of yourself." I raised my eyebrows. "Who would I beat in checkers?"

She laughed which brought on a coughing fit. I raised her head so she could breathe easier. After a while and a wipe of her face, she croaked out, "Where did you learn to lift people and raise their heads? I heard you did that for me at home too."

I shrugged.

"Maybe you should have gone into nursing?"

"No way! All that blood and stuff." I shuddered. "Gross."

"Don't make me laugh. You might have to call a real nurse. When do I get out of here?"

"They said after observation, whatever that means. Want a drink?" I slid my hand back under her head raising her and lifted the cup to her lips.

She drank and nodded. I lowered her and returned the cup to the tray. "Have they fed you?"

"Yes."

"What did they give you?"

"Lukewarm gruel and juice."

I made a face. Nasty.

"Did I make a mess in the kitchen when I went down?"

"You mean when you fell? Not too bad. I got there in time. Warren turned off the burner and we put everything into the refrigerator. I get a feast all to myself. Auntie, I need to tell you something."

She patted my hand. "What's that, dear?"

"Thank you for everything you've done for me. The shop is wonderful and I love it. You're very generous to me. I'm sorry I didn't act excited. I guess…no, I know I felt overwhelmed and frightened I'd mess it all up. This is a big undertaking for me. I've never been in charge of anything other than myself and we know how lousy I am at that."

She reached up and pushed my hair behind my ear. "Are you going to keep your hair long?"

"I don't know. Why? Does it look funny?"

"No. You are beautiful. The styles are getting shorter. I didn't know, with your new image."

I raised my eyebrows. "Image? You crack me up."

"Thank you for telling me you're scared. I can understand that. But you needn't be. You work well with your clientele and fix hair into beautiful creations. I hoped you wouldn't cut your locks."

"You're crazy worrying about my hair while you lie here. I love you."

"I love you too. Thank you for letting me treat you like a daughter. I haven't done anything for you I wouldn't have done for my child. You're my heir and I want the best for you. I love having you with me. I enjoy spoiling you. Remember when we had pizza for the first time?"

I nodded. "Best I ever had."

"Me too, because I ate it with you. You being you brings me joy. I'm sorry I didn't consult you about the shop. I got so excited to give it to you and when the idea popped into my head, I rushed full speed ahead. I realized too late how very shocked you were. I didn't mean to hurt you. You were a real trooper." She cleared her throat. "Through plunging in, learning, and hiring. Do you…"

A coughing episode interrupted her.

I helped her sit up until it calmed down.

As her breathing eased, she rested against the pillows. "Do you think you need to do anything else with staff?"

"I probably need a receptionist to answer the phone and receive people. The other girls don't seem to know how to multi-task. I'm the only one answering the phone and greeting walk-ins. I didn't realize how many walk-ins we would get. That sign you thought of was an inspiration."

"I think hiring someone is a perfect idea. Why not run an ad in the paper? As soon as I can get out of here, I'll help you weed through the applicants."

"You're not doing anything for as long as you need to get your strength up. Pneumonia is not a laughing matter."

To prove my point, she began to cough again. This time, it lasted a long while. I wiped up the spittle. "Rest. Don't talk. I'll be right back."

I sauntered until I came out into the hall then rushed to the nurse's station to demand they come in and check on her. I showed them what I had wiped up. The one with a no-nonsense attitude said, "Nurse Betty, please check on Hartford in room eleven."

I walked next to the nurse whose nametag read Betty. "My mother's name was Betty. Her sister is your patient, Mrs. Sherry Hartford. She had a few coughing spells and they seem to be getting worse. Can you please do something for her?"

She turned knowing, compassionate eyes to me and smiled. "That's my specialty. Don't worry."

Auntie appeared asleep when we came in. Betty checked her pulse and listened to her chest. Auntie stirred.

"Mrs. Hartford. How are you feeling?"

"I'm a bit tired."

"Let me help you take a drink." She did what I had done earlier. Only she made Auntie drink a bit more than I had. "I'm going to consult with the doctor and come back. You two need to say your good-byes. Visiting hours are about over and the head nurse is a stickler with rules. No sense getting her all riled up. Miss?" She peered at me.

"Carter. Jackie Carter. All right." I turned to the bed. "Auntie, I'll see you tomorrow. Sleep well." I kissed her cheek. She barely looked up, but a sweet smile graced her features.

I followed Nurse Betty out and walked with her down the hall to her station. "Thank you for taking care of her. Can you call me and let me know how she is doing tonight?"

She sighed. "Slip me your number and I'll try. It's not under my jurisdiction. The head nurse does the calls or assigns the duty nurse." She patted my hand and when I handed her the paper, she palmed it into her pocket. She checked her watch and lifted Auntie's chart and the phone in her other hand. I heard her talking to whom I assumed to be the doctor as I slipped into the stairway.

Faphick

I love it when we get to intermingle with humans and take on solid form. Jackie thought she spoke to a person named Betty, but not this time. Jackie conversed with an angel who represented a nurse. Sometimes we are allowed to appear like this so we can help in a different way. Every person in the hospital thought the angel was flesh and blood. This angel had been in their presence for months and had a unique task of demonstrating God's love and healing.

Interruption

Both Sherry and Jackie needed the angel at that particular time. The Lord on High orchestrated this interaction for a purpose only He knows.

I had volunteered but God on High had a different angel in mind. He always knows best. Contented, I watched it all and did my part by keeping the bad away from interrupting the good. I don't know the future, as I get my orders when needed. I whispered prayers on behalf of Sherry and my dear charge, Jackie.

Sherry slept while her Guardian stood watch as I followed Jackie into the hall. So many Beings flowed through the hallways of this building. Valiant Ones, as well as good and bad Beings, swarmed around people in beds and chairs, those standing, or on their way to the next World of their eternity. Fear, Loneliness, Dismay, Anger, Pain, Sickness, Disease, and others warred with the souls of humans. Meanwhile, Peace, Love, Joy, Gentleness, Calm, Hope, Patience, Healer, and others ministered. People cried, hugged others, and slept, as this unseen world played out.

Jackie left the angel whom she called Betty and proceeded out of the hospital to her aunt's car, which she had borrowed. I dutifully went with her.

Chapter 16

Jacquelyn

The phone rang and I raced to answer. "Curl Up and Dye, can I help you make an appointment? Oh, Auntie...Yes. I'll be there in a moment. Well, better give me a half hour... Perfect. I'll spring you and take you out for dinner...Love you too." I hung up and hurried to Dorothy. "Can you close up? I need to pick up Aunt Sherry from the hospital."

"Gladly."

I went to the back room for my coat and bag. I changed into my boots and dropped my shoes into my bag as I headed back to the front.

"Give her my love and tell her to rest when she gets home, and no building snow castles."

I laughed. "I'll tell her. Thanks!" I called over my shoulder. Outside, the wind had picked up and snow swirled over the sidewalk. Good old autumn in western Colorado, one minute warm and sunny, and the next, biting wind. I climbed into Auntie's car and started the engine. Although anxious to get there, I let it warm a bit.

I pulled out onto Main Street, headed east, and turned on North Seventh Street. The parking lot was full as always, but, blessed, I found a spot near the entrance. I hurried with caution, and stomped my boots free of clumps of white before I pushed the door and entered. Over to the side sat Auntie in a wheelchair. I waved and strode to her.

A Candy Striper stood behind Auntie.

I nodded to her and bent to kiss Auntie on the cheek. "Well, I see you are most anxious to get home."

"She had me push her down here as soon as she set the receiver down."

Auntie shined her best smile. "Well, no offense, but a month in here is way too long to be with even you, sweet Amanda."

"No offense taken. There are rules, though. I need you to sign this release and your niece as the responsible party does likewise." She handed a clipboard to Auntie who signed in a flourish and reached it up to me. I scanned it and I signed my name and handed it back to Amanda.

"Please pull your car up to the entrance so we can load her. Did you bring a blanket?"

"There is one in the car but it will be cold."

Interruption

"I'll get her into her coat and watch for you." Miss Candy Striper wore a take-charge expression.

Auntie rolled her eyes and I smiled before heading out into the cold. A blast pushed against me. I gasped. In the short time I was inside, the snow had piled. Men shoveled the walk as fast as snow came down. This was going to be fun.

The wind whipped my coat and my hair. I had forgotten a hat when I left this morning. I fought the wind opening the door and squeezed into the driver's side. Turning the key, the engine fired up. Warm air blasted from the vents. I hoped it heated fast.

I knew the perfectly folded blanket rested in a plastic bag under the front seat on the right side. Auntie had other supplies stashed in her car for any emergency. I wished my world were as ordered. I reached over and under, sliding it out. I pulled the blanket from its wrapper and slipped the cover back under the seat.

I eased the car toward the wide, covered waiting area and put the car into park. Scooting out, I ran to the door and the reprieve inside. Candy Striper Amanda had Auntie to the door so I only got a bit of the warmth for a nanosecond. I held the door as she wheeled Auntie out.

"Oh my!"

"I'm sorry about the weather, Aunt Sherry. I'll get you home and make you some soup and tea. No dinner out tonight," I shouted over the clamber of the wind.

Interruption

Once we were safely inside and Amanda a distance from us, I pulled away from the protection of the overhang. The roads were snow-packed and had occasional icy patches where the wind whipped the snow away.

We lived a far piece from town and the road didn't seem to have tire tracks to follow. It had grown dark and the car lamps barely lit the path. In the beam, thick white covered everything—no distinction between the road and the fields alongside. Thinking it prudent, I kept to the middle so as not to fall into a ditch.

We rounded a slight curve and a truck appeared. He swerved, as did I.

Unfortunately, that put the car in a spin. An experienced driver would instinctively know what to do. I, on the other hand, overcorrected.

Chapter 17

Jacquelyn

The car spun the other way in complete circles. I tried to right the vehicle. "Oh Lord help!"

We bumped off a wall of snow which slowed our spinning until we finally came to an abrupt stop.

Silence.

The air split in laughter.

I looked over at Auntie who laughed her fool head off. What in the world? I couldn't take it. I joined her. I realized I laughed because I'd overcome a paranoia to die in a car crash. Wasn't God amazing? We laughed and cried until a rap on the windshield startled us sober.

I rolled down the window a few inches. "Yes?"

"You all right in there?"

I peered back over my shoulder. "Aunt Sherry, you okay?"

Interruption

"I feel fine. A bit shaken but fine. Not a scrape."

I squinted at the man with the hat pulled low. "We're fine but I don't know which way we are facing and which direction is home."

"Junction is that way." He pointed. "Where you headed? I might follow to make sure you get yourselves home safe."

I glanced back at Auntie. She shrugged.

"I think we should be fine."

He bit his lip. "Lady, if you'd spun farther you'd be in the river now, freezing to death. That was some fancy driving to hit that bank at that split second. But I can't let you continue on in this blizzard by yourself." He shook his head. "Not going to be on my conscience the rest of my days. I'll turn around and lead the way. You flash your lights if you get into trouble. Turn off when you see your road and I'll wait a piece to see you make it."

"Thank you." I cranked up the window.

He lumbered away.

"What do you think?" I strained to see her in the dark. How had I seen him so clearly and yet could hardly make out Sherry's features?

"I think we need to trust him. Apparently you're a fantastic driver but I don't want to test those skills again tonight."

"All right." I waited until he passed and pulled onto his tracks. "Why do you think a dump truck is out here in a blizzard?"

"I don't know, but his tracks are easy to follow."
"They sure are."

Faphick

God on High sent more angels to help these women during the snowstorm and kept the car on the road. Beings were determined to disrupt their lives and we Valiant Ones had our weapons in full swing.

Swarming inside and out of the car were Fear, Worry, Tension, and Anxiety, while Peace, Calm, Patience, and Trust were called upon by Sherry. The battle started against both Sherry and Jackie but when the Beings realized they had already lost with Sherry, they concentrated all their efforts on Jackie.

God dispatched an angel to drive a truck. At first, I didn't understand why the truck got in the way.

Then it all became clear.

The car needed to be completely out of control. The women needed to see they couldn't fix this. Only God on High had the power.

After Jackie's simple prayer for help, Fear, Worry, and Anxiety took to the sidelines. Trust captured the lead. Peace, Calm, and Patience coaxed and applauded.

Sherry and Jackie were flooded with Peace after Jackie and Sherry released Tension in the laughter brought on by Joy.

Following the tracks made by the truck, they felt safer and made it without incident. Jackie's mind swam with questions. I smiled at her normal reaction to things unseen. The most important thing that happened—Jackie's prayer. Prayer disrupts evil and ignites the Holy Spirit to work in the person.

I understood how quickly things might change. Jackie could remain with Truth, Calm, and Peace flooding her soul. Or, she could give in to Worry.

Jacquelyn

The car didn't slip as I drove in the tracks left by the dump truck. After a few miles, our driveway came into view. Auntie's voice interrupted my worrying. "I hope the car can make it through the deep snow to the garage. I don't want to trudge through this stuff."

"My thoughts exactly. I hope we don't get stuck."

"I've been praying since we left the hospital. I feel God is taking care of us."

I peered into the rearview mirror expecting to see the dump truck turn around.

Darkness.

"The lights from the dump truck are gone."

"They went off right after you turned. You don't think he broke down, do you?"

"Right now, I just want to concentrate on driving."

I anticipated the curve in the driveway and took it without difficulty. Only a few bumps and a slight fishtail, as we climbed the rise until we arrived safe and sound. I popped out to knee-deep snow to open the garage door. I trudged back and parked in the clean, dry garage. "Thank you, Jesus!"

"Yes! And good job, Jackie. Let's go in and warm up."

I jumped out and pulled the giant door down against the storm and hurried to help her into the house. Although she didn't seem to need my assistance, she let me do the motherly act.

Boots and coats off, I set the water on for tea, pulled soup I previously made out of the refrigerator, and placed the pot on medium to heat. Curious, I went to the window in the front room to check on the truck. I couldn't find it. If his lights were on, I would have seen them. He must have taken off while we were out of sight of the road. That would've been impossibly fast driving. Our house sat high on a hill overlooking the valley and no lights appeared on the road in either direction.

Auntie placed her hand on my shoulder. "Jackie, I don't think we will ever find that truck or its driver."

I swiveled. "Why?"

"I feel we've had an encounter with one of God's messengers. An angel. The Bible speaks of us entertaining angels. I think that lovely man was indeed an angel. Think about it. What do you remember about him?"

"His persistence, and there seemed an aura about him. I saw him clearly even in the darkness."

She nodded. "I noticed that, too. He drew particular attention to your fancy driving and the split second we hit the snowbank. How would you describe your driving?"

"Terrible. I over-reacted and over compensated. I didn't drive steady until we followed the tire impressions and then here on our driveway."

"After you called out to the Lord, everything seemed to work better."

She had given me a lot to chew on. That cry for help came instinctively and calmed me—a new experience for me. I headed to the kitchen. "The soup needs stirring."

Soon the soup steamed and I ladled the savory meal into bowls while Auntie fixed our tea.

She set the teacups on the table and perched on a chair. I carried the bowls and crackers over and joined her.

She clasped my hand. "Lord, thank You again for getting us home safely. Whether that man was one of your angels or a Good Samaritan, I believe You led him there. Thank You, for this food and our time we have with one another on this snowy night. In Jesus's name, Amen."

She lifted her spoon and blew on a bite. "Why are you smiling?"

"I am amazed how much I've learned in a short amount of time. The Lord seems personal to me now. I don't feel like a frightened and crushed girl anymore."

"I agree. Your transformation is remarkable."

I got up and gave her a much-needed hug. "Thank you." We continued our conversation between bites of chicken, rice, and vegetable soup.

"We need each other and can learn from each other. My faith has grown too because of you."

I raised my eyebrow. "Maybe spending time at the hospital in an oxygen tent had something to do with it."

"Yes. Solitude helps you speak to the only One there. I realized how fragile life can be. And believe me, I want to make the most of the time I have left."

"I do too. Auntie, I still don't know what God desires for me to do."

"I think you're already doing it. Your patrons seem pleased and your appointment calendar is full."

"I enjoy my occupation. Dorothy, Ellen, and Kathrine are pleasant to work with, and the ladies who come in are unique and fun. Still, I felt Jesus had something more in mind."

"Keep praying about it and be open to His leading."

"That's what I'm trying to do."

"He will show you."

Chapter 18

Jacquelyn

Prof Frankie leaned back and brought his right ankle up to rest on his left knee. This pose had become familiar. He thought it gave an illusion of a calm and easygoing nature. I referred to his posture as his warrior stance. He didn't fool me.

I braced myself.

"Jackie, how is the beauty shop?

"Really well, thank you. I enjoy my work and the clientele. The women who work with me are wonderful. We function as a flawless four-person tap dance routine, never out of step." I sipped my bold, dark brew of tea.

"I'm pleased it's going so well. How is your relationship with Warren?"

"I'm sure you've heard we're going steady." I pulled out the chain holding Warren's class ring. "See?"

He grinned. Amazing. I didn't get many of those from him even though we have had so many breakthroughs and he now acted as if he may like me. What was his agenda?

"What is on your heart that you are praying for?"

Boom! Just like that, a bullseye. He shot that arrow straight and true.

I set my teacup on the table. Better to have my hands free of distraction as I navigated.

"Oh, you know, the normal things—Auntie, Warren, his practice, full bookings at my shop, etc. Do you need me to pray for you?" Ha. Got ya.

"That would be nice. Thank you. I pray for you."

Swoop. The arrow flew. He didn't miss.

"I didn't know that. Do you pray for all your patients or only those who have the most to deal with?"

"All of them. I go over my schedule daily and pray for them. When the Lord lays people on my mind, I pray for them right then. Lately, you've often come to mind. So, I want to know what you are wrestling with God about."

His aim was sure. I cleared my throat.

Tick. Tick. Oh brother, the infernal clock has to give its two cents' worth. *Tick. Tick.*

"What job did God give me to do? Why me? What could I possibly do for Him? I'm a dancer who can't dance who went into beauty school. What can a beautician do for Christ? I don't get it."

"What do you think He wants?"

"Really, didn't you hear me? I don't know."

"When you pray, what nudging do you feel?"

"It's confusing."

"Talk it out. How so?"

"When I ask Him what He wants, in my mind, I get a flash of my shop with women in the chairs. I'm in the middle, talking, but I don't know what I'm saying. Then, in my mind, I see Jesus with His hand on my shoulder saying, "You need to go back. I have work for you." Then it fades. What does He mean?"

"What do you think it means?"

I shrugged.

"Jackie, where are you in the vision?"

"In my shop."

"Doing?"

"Talking."

"You know what you've been called to do."

"What, hold church services in my shop?"

"Not in the conventional way. What message could you give? What is the last thing you see?"

"Jesus in Heaven."

"Yes. Put them together."

Tick. Tick.

My hand flew to cover my face. "I can't do that! I don't know how. I'm insignificant. A dancer turned hairdresser. What do I know? I'm not a preacher."

A tear slid. I wiped it away. Why that?

"Did He tell you to go to school for that?"

I shook my head.

"Did He say to preach?"

"No."

"How did you feel when He put His hand on your shoulder and told you He had a job for you?"

"I felt needed, loved, confident…"

"You are those things."

Really? I was? *Tick. Tick.*

"What is the most exciting thing you've experienced in your life?"

It hit me. The arrow he shot, split the other arrow in the bullseye.

"God wants me to talk about Him? At the shop?"

"What do you think?"

I closed my eyes as realization cemented itself into my soul. "How?"

"I imagine you only need to talk about what you know and have experienced. He will give you the words."

I looked at Prof Frankie. "You think so?"

"What else did Jesus Christ say to you when He said good-bye?"

I closed my eyes and focused on hearing His voice. "He said, 'I will go with you and help you, never to forsake you. You won't see me but my presence is always there.'"

I looked up and said, "Oh, and I only needed to call on Him."

"Yes. He will never forsake you. You don't need to be afraid. Call on Him. Try it out. Speak to your clients while you fix their hair and see what happens."

I picked up my tea and swallowed the last of it.

"You've been afraid and that's why you didn't want to acknowledge what you already knew. How do you feel now?"

"Relieved that I know, but scared to death."

"Anytime we go out of our comfort zone, we will be afraid. God teaches us when we are uncomfortable. Never stop being uncomfortable. Learn and grow. Step out in faith. Are you willing to step out in obedience, in faith?"

I took a deep breath. Was I? *Tick. Tick.* "Yes. I am. I don't know what it looks like, but I am."

"He will show you because He asked you to do it."

Yes. All I had to do was take that first step. Frankie said to try it out. "What have I got to lose?"

"Trepidation."

"Right." I peered at my companion who hung on the wall—the one shouting the seconds and prodding me to speak. Time. I didn't know how much time I had in this life, so I had better make good use of it. I stood. "Thanks again. The Lord must talk to you—otherwise you have a reel-to-reel in my closet recording my prayers."

He laughed. "I would never invade your privacy. I only ask questions and they lead to you being astonished at your own answers. Remember, we are not alone in these meetings. The Holy Spirit is working in you and in me. The Lord said where 'two or more are gathered in my name,' He would be there. I try to listen to the Holy Spirit's prodding. The more we listen, the easier it is to hear Him speak. I know you are learning this and it is evident in your life. Don't be surprised that we have breakthroughs, tears, revelations, and hope for a brighter tomorrow. I think we can again lengthen the time in between sessions. You've done well having one every other month, how about once a quarter?"

"I've graduated?"

"Yes, and sometime you will get a diploma."

"You're trying to charm me with humor? Thank you?"

Faphick

I loved watching the match between Dr. Franks and Jackie. She thought she moved the target, but his questions were true to what she equated as an arrow hitting a bullseye. Every session became easier to get to the problem because her heart had been softening to the Lord. The Holy Spirit in him worked in his spirit as the Holy Spirit in her spoke to her spirit and her soul.

My job, while Jackie struggled in the office, intensified. Many Beings attacked her. Lately, she carried Fear around her. Fear pulled her back while she struggled to move forward. Trepidation, Doubt, and Anxiety were constant companions. Each sneered Discouragement's words into her mind, will, and emotions. She started to believe their lies. As they became familiar, she clung to them.

In the session, the Beings grew impatient to be heard—the last-ditch effort on their part to overcome her and make her impotent to share Love's message of the gospel. I swatted and poked at them with my sword, trying to keep them busy with me so they would loosen their hold. I was reminded it was her choice to reject them or accept them. I only did what God on High told me to do.

She managed to shrug off Doubt. Then, one by one, she pushed the fallen Beings away as she was emboldened by Confidence, Assurance, Peace, and Understanding. She accepted overflowing Love and embraced her calling. As she let go of each Being, I let them feel the edge of my sword on their way out to lick their wounds.

Songs of Praise flowed from Heaven to Earth and back as the angelic hosts sang there and here.

Chapter 19

1958
Jacquelyn

A short time after Aunt Sherry got out of the hospital, she became my full-time receptionist at *Curl up and Dye*.

One day, she came in with an electric percolator and the place changed. I ended up buying two benches to add to the existing two in my waiting room. I shouldn't call it a waiting room. While they waited, women were treated to tea and cookies—Auntie's idea.

I remember the day very clearly. "Aunt Sherry, what do you have there?" I pointed to the chrome appliance in her hand.

"I think we need to set up refreshments for our clientele, so I bought this to heat water for tea."

I frowned. "Why? They seem to hang out here already. I don't get it. When their hair and nails are finished, they stay. Don't people have other places to be?"

"Women don't sit here to wait for appointments, although they do. They come and stay to listen." She smiled.

"Listen?" My frown deepened. "Not for a haircut?"

"Yes, honey. Don't you realize they come to hear you talk? You give them hope and strengthen their faith."

I felt my face crunch up. "What are you talking about?"

Auntie shook her head. "You really don't know." She took me by the hand and pulled me over to push me into her chair. "Flip through the appointment book and read the names."

I slid my finger down the time slots on the days for the month, and then it hit me. "We have repeats more often than the normal time for a style to be needing a comb-out, or cut."

"Exactly. They come to hear you talk about Heaven and what you've learned."

I stewed over what she said. This might be the calling, the "Go" that Jesus sent me to do. "I did what Prof Frankie said, and tested and prayed. I talked about what I knew. When fear had crowded me, I prayed and felt the Lord give me the words to say. I just didn't realize the impact of what I did. I thought I only told my experience in Heaven, my salvation, my sinful escapades, forgiveness, and growth. Thank you, Auntie, for believing in me and giving me this place. Just keep praying I don't blow it or back down."

She hugged me. "I do and will."

Faphick

The coming and going of people, Guardians, and Beings into the shop impressed me. Had they all been in bodily form, there wouldn't be enough room to move. As it were, I brandished my sword when needed. God on High had created us with a perception that humans don't have. I sensed Beings and people as friend or foe before they crowded into the room, and I stood ready.

My charge drew these people like flies to a piece of over-ripe fruit. People brought Beings with them—some for edification and some for corruption.

Jackie didn't know what impact she had on the people and the Beings as well. She frustrated many Beings to the point of fleeing. A few shrewd ones stopped before crossing the threshold and didn't enter, having recognized the atmosphere for what it had become. Calm, Peace, Rest, Companionship, Prudence, Patience, Gentleness,

Interruption

Empathy, Joy, Fulfillment, Contentment, and others flitted around and swarmed through the place, in and around the humans.

A few of the humans came in with weights of Beings affixed to them. Corruption, Ill Will, Deception, Depravity, Lawlessness, Laxness, Laziness, Bitterness, and Fear played mind games, pricked, and prodded their hosts.

A few wicked Beings came by themselves with the hope to latch on to a human. Unfortunately, sometimes they were successful.

Strong people listened to the wise words of Jackie and took Courage's advice and kicked evil Beings out of their life, or stopped them before they could grab on. At those times, Cheer and Praise raised their voices, resounding in high decibels.

All this took place because Jackie had listened to the call of the Father for His child to speak of Him and His Heaven. To talk of God's love and forgiveness. To whisper words of wisdom and encouragement. And most importantly—share the Gospel of Salvation. Jackie had known Suffering, Brokenness, Anger, and Devastation, for they had clung to her, causing untold Grief and ruin her life, inciting death. God intervened and she lived. Jackie grew strong and remembered her salvation. Through the godly council, she had changed her mindset to look for Good around her, and Wholesome God-focused thoughts became the norm.

Interruption

Jacquelyn

I teased Jean's hair into a stylish bouffant as I recounted my visit to Heaven. I acquired the ability to relive my experience while concentrating on a hair creation. "Heaven is the most exquisite and perfect place where every amazing feel-good emotion swirled through my being and my senses were tantalized. My eyes wanted to soak in everything from the spectacular colors around me to the beauty and detail of my Lord's face.

"The feel of the grass on my toes and the warmth of the gold path delighted my feet. The velvet softness of a flower's petal felt amazing in my fingers. Oh my goodness, the fragrance lingered in my nostrils even as I left the glorious place."

I sprayed stiffening hairspray over her hair. "Smell that? Pretty bad, isn't it? We talk about how things smell, whether good or bad. Delightful or awful. In Heaven, it smells clean. Fragrances from flowers, grass, trees, fruit, and even the wind carried crisp, yet warm, clean balms which are the most pleasant scents I've ever enjoyed.

"I couldn't believe the taste of the fruit. I have no idea the kind of fruit nor have I ever savored anything close to its goodness. This is the size of it." I made a sphere of my hands with my fingers spread and about four inches from one hand to the other. "About the size of a cantaloupe, only from a tree."

I brushed off the cape across Jean's shoulders. Untying the neck, I slipped it off to shake it free of fallen hair. Grabbing the broom, I proceeded to sweep the dark locks that I'd cut off. "Melodic voices of people, birds, water, the rustle of the leaves on the trees in the wind, and His voice caressed my hearing. Not only the sound but what my loved ones said and He said resonated into my soul. My momma gave me her love. It flowed all over me. Said she was proud of me. I didn't know at the time, but my guide happened to be my Lord, Jesus Christ. Although, my spirit knew because of how He made me feel. I experienced inexplicable peace, joy, trust, and fulfillment all wrapped up in His lovingkindness which the Bible, in Hebrew, calls *hesed*, completely encompassed around and through me.

"What I remember most is what He said. He told me I had a job yet to do. What He meant baffled me for years."

Jean stood and patted my shoulder. "Honey, you are helping people. We come here to get away from our cares for a spell. We can see Heaven through your eyes and descriptions—very vivid, I might add. We can then look forward to the wonderful place God is preparing for us. We can get through another day, and another week, knowing our security is in Him. I've heard you as you clearly explain the gospel, how Jesus came and died on the cross taking our sin on Himself and shedding His blood to pay for our sin. He rose again and He is right now preparing a place for us! Amen and Halleluiah!" She went to Auntie and paid her bill and left humming "Amazing Grace."

Faphick

The dream started pleasantly. Jackie's dreams of Heaven always were. In her dream, she scanned the faces of her loved ones. Love flowed between them. Then she searched them again, sweeping her eyes over her mother and those around her. Jackie's heart beat faster and faster. She broke out in a sweat. Her body thrashed back and forth. This wonderful calming dream had turned. I knew someday this would happen. Praise the Lord, another break of understanding would soon follow.

I left Agitation and Bewilderment alone to do what they did best. Fear crouched close, ready to pounce if given the opportunity.

Peace and Comfort waited until accepted.

"Jackie, it will be all right," I sang to her.

Devastation jumped into the fray.

That did it.

Chapter 20

Jacquelyn

My wailing woke me and Auntie rushed into my room. "Honey, what's wrong. Are you sick?"

In a split second, she held me as I cried into her shoulder. "He's not there! Auntie, he isn't there. I'd know him, right? I would. I know I would. But he isn't there."

"Who? Who isn't where? Calm down and start at the beginning."

"I dreamt of Heaven, and while I'm talking to my loved ones I realized Dad isn't there. Aunt Sherry, He isn't in Heaven! How can that be?"

"Oh, sweetheart. I'm so sorry. I didn't think about him not being there. But it makes sense."

I lifted my head. "What? Please tell me."

She tugged a tissue out of the box and handed it to me. "It's almost morning. Come to the kitchen, I'll make tea

150

and we will talk. Bring your Bible." Auntie got up and went toward the kitchen. Confused, saddened, and agitated, I followed, almost afraid of what she would tell me.

I pulled out a chair and sat at the table in her perfectly organized kitchen. She once had said, "I want to be able to make myself a cup of tea without turning on a light." Well, she hadn't turned on one and frankly, I didn't want light now either. Maybe this was a dream inside a dream? I could only hope. Why, Lord?

Choices.

Choices? I don't understand. Only a few times had I heard His voice inside my soul. I wish He talked to me more often and in longer sentences.

Auntie placed a spoon and honey in front of me. "It will be ready in a moment. While we wait, tell me how God made us. Did He make us as robots to do His bidding?"

"Of course not. He made us with a free will. Oh." I nodded. "Choices. We choose to believe."

The kettle sang. She lifted it and poured hot water into two white china cups. She carried them to the table as I waited for her to continue.

I grabbed the tin with assorted teas and selected the strongest black tea in the lot and dropped it into my cup. I drizzled honey in and stirred, then I swirled the teabag around, dunking it up and down.

"Your daddy loved your momma and he loved you. I highly respected him as one of the most caring persons I knew and a good man. He treated people with respect and dignity. He was a kind and loving man who felt he didn't do anything bad enough to go to hell over. He thought he was good enough. No matter how many times your momma, the pastor, myself, or your uncle tried to explain that we are all born with sin, he said he didn't do anything wrong. He said he never told a lie or stole a cent. He never swore or hit your mom. He respected his parents and the law. So he, on his own merit, should be granted Heaven."

I frowned. "No one is perfect." I took a scalding gulp for fortification.

"True. He refused to admit he had a flaw, a pride issue. Although a kind man, he felt a bit above the rest of us. He wouldn't take any handouts. Would rather starve himself and let his family suffer from inadequate food, clothing, and shoes. World War I took its toll on him and his family. His dad accepted food from families who had more and shared with others less fortunate, but your dad resented that. He looked down on his dad for getting in that mess in the first place. Your dad forgot we were a community and we all helped each other. No one but your dad felt bad about sharing and helping and accepting what others had to give.

"He never raised his voice or showed anger, but your uncle and I felt he let anger fester inside. The pride and anger monsters took up residence in his heart. I believe that's why he died of a heart attack. He bottled up everything inside and one day it erupted."

"Why didn't Momma tell me?"

"Honey, your momma wanted you to think well about your dad. She wanted you to have good thoughts, not be plagued with bad."

"Oh, Auntie, he didn't choose God. He didn't choose eternal life in Heaven with Jesus and all of us. This is so sad and breaks my heart." Tears trailed down my cheeks.

"God didn't want your dad to choose the way he did. But He created him as He made all of us, with a free will to choose Him or reject Him. Not everyone is on his or her way to Heaven. Some choose to reject Jesus Christ and what He did on the cross for us. This is why I am so pleased you are sharing the Lord and His love to everyone who comes into the shop. Have you noticed, husbands are arriving early to hear you speak? Ladies are getting fewer hairstyles that need drying time under the loud hoods? They want to hear your message of eternal life. Love is what you speak of and love is what you demonstrate. This is your calling. I believe it is what the Lord meant when He said your work wasn't finished. What does Warren say about it?" She sipped her tea.

"I told him, but not the way you make it out to be. You elaborate and make it sound more than I think it is. Anyway, thank you for telling me. I'm sad and sorry I won't see my dad. I'm going to pray harder for some of the ones who are still on the fence. I want everyone to go to Heaven. It's so glorious. Every day, I feel blessed that God gave me the gift of dying and giving me a tour of Heaven and sending me back for His purpose."

"He could have kept you and we wouldn't have the blessing of you and your descriptions and recounting of Heaven. Or worse, He could have left you on Earth never having experienced Heaven."

I jerked my eyes to hers. I had never thought of that. I lowered my head and squeezed my eyes shut. "Thank You, Jesus, for taking me to Heaven. Help me use that gift every day of my life."

"Amen."

She stretched. "What are your plans today?"

"I have a date with Warren after church."

"Good. I plan on taking a nap."

I laughed. "Sorry for waking you so early. Thanks for being there for me."

"I appreciate having you here. Won't be long now, and you'll be married."

She had an uncanny way of knowing things beforehand. I could only hope and pray she was right.

Jacquelyn

Warren held my hand as we walked to his car. He bent down and spoke softly in my ear. "You're beautiful. A new dress?"

I felt the heat. I hated blushing and he always knew how to bring one flaming up my neck and cheeks. I ducked my head. "Yes. Ellen and I went shopping. I bought a few things."

We arrived at his car and he unlocked the door. "You chose well." Warren opened it for me to climb in. He closed the door and sprung around to his side. I slid over to sit close. I loved the way he smelled and being near him.

He grinned as he lowered himself into the driver's side. "You've been spending a lot of time with Ellen and I'm glad she's your friend. Any preference where you want to go for lunch?"

I shook my head. "No. You choose."

"I have a perfect place but I need to stop by the house first."

"All right." The drive took less than three minutes. He bumped the car up the driveway and left the engine running as he dashed inside his house. I liked his bungalow style house which he had moved into a few months ago. I helped him pick some of the furniture for it. The house was a bit sparse but comfortable. I had only been inside a few times. We mostly met in public, so tongues wouldn't wag. At least that's what we said out loud. I knew in my heart the spark we felt could ignite into a bonfire real quick if we were alone.

The screen door banged shut and he scooted down the three steps, carrying a picnic basket. He plopped it into the back seat and jumped back in. The car roared out the driveway and headed out of town. "That's sweet. You know how much I love to eat outdoors with you. Are you taking me to our spot?"

His grin widened showing his cute dimple. "You bet."

His face became serious. "Jackie, I feel something is bothering you. Can you tell me?"

"That noticeable?"

"To me it is."

"I'm glad you know me well. Last night I had a horrific dream. My sobbing woke me. In the early hours, Auntie and I had a long talk. I'm afraid my dad isn't in Heaven. He never chose to accept God's free gift of salvation. He wouldn't humble himself. He thought he was good enough. That's like trying to jump off the Grand Canyon rim to the other side. I've not been there but I've seen pictures—an impossible feat."

He took my hand. "Sweetheart, I'm sorry. That must be devastating. What are your thoughts going forward?"

Interruption

"Share God and the gospel more fervently. I think God revealed this to me to prod me into action, not to wallow in what I can't change. I can be sad and dismayed but I need to look ahead, like you said, forward. Keep moving forward."

"That's my girl. You have come a long way." He squeezed my hand before letting go to turn the car into the parking lot.

The park had a trail that led into the bluffs where we loved to sit and gaze at the view. I smoothed out my dark yellow skirt. I hoped it wouldn't get dirty.

Warren found a parking space. As usual, we weren't the only ones. He jumped out and reached for my hand. Taking it, I scooted out his side. He unlocked the trunk and came back with the sack holding a pair of tennis shoes I kept in his car. We frequently walked here and I would be in need of a change of shoes. Some things about Auntie were wearing off on me. I sat on the bumper and slipped them on. Also inside the sack were two blankets, one to sit on, and one to wrap around my skirt. I tied the red one around my waist. I gave him the sack with my heels inside and he placed them in the trunk.

Warren held the basket and grabbed my hand. "Come on, fair lass."

Chapter 21

Jacquelyn

I led the way up the narrow footpath, worn smooth from centuries of travelers. Warren told me the Ute Indians once lived in these mountainous bluffs. I imagined I walked in the same path as an Indian family. The brave led the way. His squaw, with a baby strapped on her back, holding the hands of two more children, followed close behind. Neither an adult nor child made a noise as they blazed their trail through the wilderness.

I came around a large outcropping of sandstone and found the area we loved. In spring and early summer, grass, small delicate flowers, and sagebrush brought color to the barren brown and red landscape. A shallow creek flowed down to the river below. Today, the fall sun warmed the ground. Dry grass and dead leaves crunched under our shoes. The creek held a shallow flow from early snow that had melted. Indian summer had come to us to warm the day.

A few other groups of people were also enjoying the warm autumn day. I found a spot a bit away from the others and spread out the blue checked blanket and sat down. Warren lowered himself next to me.

"I'm starved, what did you bring for us to eat?"

He chuckled. "You, my love, are always starved. Where you put it, I don't know. What you'd expect—fried chicken, potato salad, green beans, rolls, and two slices of pie. At least that's what I bribed my mom into making. Otherwise, it would have been sandwiches. There should be a thermos of lemonade too."

I reached up and kissed his cheek. "Yippee!"

He laughed at my enthusiasm and leaned back on his elbows while I unpacked the basket. My mouth watered thinking about his mom's cooking. My momma had no way to teach me. Traveling on the train or bus and staying in motel rooms didn't present an opportunity. What little I knew, I'd learned from Auntie.

I pulled out two large flat bowls covered in foil. Two sets of utensils wrapped in napkins and a thermos came out next. I saw two smaller containers that must have held the pieces of pie. "Ready?"

Warren sat up, reached for my hand, and prayed. His respectful and tender prayer touched my heart.

"Go ahead and dig in." He uncovered his dish and lifted his fork but waited for me to take a bite.

I picked up a chicken leg and sunk my teeth into the crunchy, tender meat. Yep, the woman could cook.

In between bites, I asked, "Bribed with what?"

"I told her I'd clear out my stuff from the attic."

"When?"

"Friday afternoon. Want to come?"

"Yes. I'd love to see all your childhood memorabilia. It may shed light."

"Light?" He lifted his brow. "What are you getting at?"

I commanded my face to be as free of emotion as I possibly could. "Your interests and the things you collected is all. Honest."

"Yeah, right. I see the wheels spinning in that pretty head of yours. You want to know if I was a bookworm and a backward boy. I'll have you know there's some cool stuff."

"You mean, among the encyclopedias and dictionaries?"

"Wait and see." He wiggled his eyebrows.

I smiled.

"You're finished all ready?"

"What?"

He pointed his fork at my plate. "Your plate is practically licked clean." My eyes widened and I sucked my lips into my mouth. He'd caught me again. He laughed.

I grinned. No sense denying it. I could put it away faster than a rattlesnake could strike.

"Go ahead and pick your pie." He nodded toward the basket.

I peered under the wrappings and grabbed the apple and left the pecan for Warren. His mother always made two pies every other week. Either they'd have company or she'd bring one to a neighbor. I believed the woman didn't need a reason but loved to bake and cook.

I savored the first tangy-sweet, delectable bite. Almost as good as Heaven. No, not quite, but very good. Her crusts were always a perfect texture. Do I dare ask her to teach me to cook and bake? I bit my lip.

"Not to your liking?"

"What? Oh. No, it's fantastic."

"What were you thinking?"

"Remember the first time we went on a date and I finished before you had a fourth of yours eaten?"

"Yes. That's when I fell in love with you."

"Really? Why?"

"Because you felt comfortable enough to devour your food and not worry about propriety."

"Interesting. I felt a bit awkward after I realized what I'd done."

"I know, and that made it all the more special. You didn't conform to society's rules."

"Society rules for me meant fight for everything. Finish first or starve. Do the best, arrive first, sweat the most, and sleep the least. Dog eat dog. Wars. The stage is filled with Pollyannas and divas."

He put his hand over mine. "Sweetheart, I'm glad you don't have those battles anymore."

"I do. Battles exist but you, we, cannot see them. I fight myself all the time. My insecurities and old wounds surface, causing tension, grief, self-loathing, doubts, procrastination, fear." I splayed my hands. "You name it."

"You're right. We all have those to deal with. Some more so than others. I have those battles too."

"You do?"

"Yes."

"Like now. I doubt I have what it takes to make a difference in people's lives. To build my practice where it needs to be. To do all the rest I want to do with my life. You, my darling girl, have your shop and ladies flock to it. You're booked solid. I see a huge future in front of you. The buzz around town." He waved his palm across the sky. "Amazing lady runs beauty shop on Main Street."

I blushed.

Warren took my empty plate and set it on the blanket. "So amazing, in fact…" He pulled me to my feet and took a knee. "I would be honored if you would become my wife. Will you, Jacquelyn Francis Carter, marry me?" In his hand, a box with a sparkling ring appeared.

My head had a hard time taking in what my ears clearly heard. Wife? Me?

"Oh! Yes! Yes, I will marry you!"

He stood and picked me up and swung me around. I giggled.

I heard cheering from the picnicking people I'd forgotten were there.

He set me down and tenderly kissed me. The kiss soared my emotions to the sky. My heart raced. My body quaked. Marriage. Auntie had been right. Again. Good.

Faphick

I never understood why the fallen Beings wanted to mess with humans so much. Their hatred of God on High must consume them. They don't want anyone to follow the Lord. They act as if humans are their toys. They annoy them until they are broken, downtrodden, weak, and useless.

People let Beings provoke them. The followers of God on High are given a way to get through trials and come out shining brighter than they did when the Beings attacked. If a person allows, the Lord gives grace and the Holy Spirit leads them through the flames of trials.

Those who chose not to believe in God on High and trust His Son Jesus Christ could become puppets of the Beings.

Used for their devious schemes. If only they would cry out to God on High. He was always waiting and desired all to come to Him and worship Him.

Jackie and Warren were special in God's eyes. He loved all His children and every one of them was special. The Beings sensed that these two had something important to do for the Lord. They watched, analyzed, and attacked at every weak moment.

Warren's Guardian, Whaxgum, and I were on full alert to protect and combat outside influences as Jackie and Warren walked hand-in-hand. Their young, untried love for each other grew every day. Pride tried to weasel into each of their thoughts.

Lately, Sensuousness and Lust tickled and poked at their senses, prodding them to cave into Desire. Warren and Jackie loved each other and the normal physical reaction had been heightened to a thunderous roar. These two worked hard at stifling the urges because they knew they should wait until they made their covenant before man and God on High.

Warren planned his proposal and picked the perfect spot with people around them, yet semi-alone. Jackie had no idea he had saved money for months and debated for hours at a jewelry store to pick the perfect diamond ring to slip on her finger.

God-honoring Beings cheered them on, but the others sneered for their defeat. The battle lines were drawn and temptation would increase. Whaxgum caught my eye. I nodded. I swung my sword in an arc as he did, to remind evil that God on High ruled supreme.

Chapter 22

Jacquelyn

Giggling and out of breath, we sank to our knees on the blanket. "I had no idea." I shook my head. "You surprised me." I gazed into his beautiful eyes. Did he see the love flowing from mine?

"Can we set the date? And get married soon?" His eyes grew large with what I assumed to be anticipation.

"Warren, Auntie will want to give me a huge wedding and that will take months to put together." I rested my hand on his chest. "But I'll try to rein her in." I smiled. "Sweetheart, don't worry, it will happen soon."

"Not soon enough." I saw a flicker of concern cross his face.

I helped him fold the blanket and we headed to the car. I felt our relationship had changed and shifted, becoming stronger as if we were two magnets drawn toward each other. An overwhelming sense of certainty came over me and I knew we would have to fight to keep purity at the forefront.

I felt his hand more acutely than I had as we walked up this path. His arm brushed my side as he helped me over a rough spot and a sizzle rippled through me. How could a simple engagement change everything? I hoped I could persuade Auntie to agree on a short timeline. I had been told a little of how a man felt physically when attracted to a woman and knew it could be stronger than what a woman might feel. My focus shifted as I became extremely tuned into him and I realized I had my work cut out for me. We loved and respected each other. Sex before marriage was out of the question, but would we be strong enough to stay the course?

"Do you remember our first alone date?" Warren interrupted my thoughts.

"On the train or when you sprung for the nice Italian restaurant downtown?"

"I was referring to the latter. But the first one seemed nice too."

"I remember everything about it. What we ate, our waiter, music, what we wore, the breadsticks, the lasagna, and the dessert."

He laughed. "You spoke of the food twice. Do you remember what we talked about?"

"Yes. We talked about significant things in our lives. Your favorite teachers, my favorite dance moves. You almost made me get up and show you."

"You blushed and I got a bad crush on you."

"You did?"

"Yes."

At the car, I changed my shoes, and positioned myself in the car near Warren.

He turned the key to the on position, pushed the ignition button, and the car roared into life. "Honey, don't get embarrassed when you blush. It's endearing. Sweet and pretty. What else did we talk about?"

"I told you about my accident and Heaven."

Warren drove the car up the rise in the driveway to Auntie's and my house. "That's when I knew you were special. God had done an incredible thing for you. I wanted to know you more."

"But then."

"Yes. Then."

He parked. "You drew away from me."

"That's because I didn't want you to know the bad stuff."

"When you finally told me, I felt so sorry for you but relieved you had faced the past."

"Prof Frankie knew he needed to be extremely tough on me. I'm a hard nut to crack. He made all the emotions erupt so I could voice my fears. He picked and prodded until I let it out about my momma and feeling it was my fault she left and died before I had a chance to tell her I loved her." I placed my hand on his arm. "I want to tell you again, thank you for giving Auntie his name. I heard you had to pull some strings so he would fit me into his schedule."

"I'm glad I did. He's a great guy and one I've looked up to for years. He taught a class I took, which solidified my decision to go into the same field. I hope and pray every day that I might be a fraction of the caliber of counselor he is."

"You will."

We sat in companionable silence for a moment.

"Warren." I placed my hand on his arm. "He taught me about armor. He shared what Ephesians 6 talks about. Our battle we fight isn't against people but against a host we cannot see. They use weapons to pierce our thoughts and emotions. They can deceive and malign. We need to put on the Armor of God. We need to saturate ourselves in His Word and speak to Him in prayer all throughout our day. Anytime a skewed thought comes, we need to fight it off. Using Scripture is the best way, but always asking the Holy Spirit's help and guidance will stop the immediate attack."

"Yes. We need to be vigilant and wary. Satan and his followers' attacks sneak upon us. These talks are good. Thank you for sharing your struggles and what you've learned. I want us to talk deeply and about frivolous things. I hope to share all your life. I'll want to hear the plans for our wedding. Sweetheart, let's go in and tell your Aunt Sherry our good news."

"Seems that we will be telling your parents as well." I pointed at the car coming over the rise.

We said, "Auntie" at the same time. Warren burst out in laughter and I joined him. Yes, she seemed to know things before they were anything. She probably invited them over for the news before Warren proposed.

Faphick

When people who trust God on High come together, Valiant Ones get to ease off. Five of us, five people who love the Lord, and dozens of God-honoring Beings make for a pleasant atmosphere.

Jackie and Warren were congratulated and Jackie proudly moved her hand so the light sparkled off the engagement ring for all to see. They celebrated as did we. God on High opened the window of Heaven for His love and light to flow freely into their dwelling and their souls. The human's spirits rose in praise for the Lord.

Aunt Sherry and Warren's parents proclaimed God's blessings over the couple. Peace, Prosperity, Commitment, Honesty, Forbearance, and Patience echoed the words.

Warren's dad, Eugene, prayed over the couple and the souls of the others united with his words.

For this moment in earthly time, perfect love flowed between the five adults. I knelt and prayed this would last their lifetime. God hadn't told me otherwise but I had guarded thousands of humans and understood these times only lasted for brief periods.

Wisdom told me long ago, acknowledge this and be prepared. The Guardians understood and urged our charges to heed Wisdom.

Chapter 23

1959
Jacquelyn

I slipped on the new black patent leather shoes that were as comfortable as dance shoes. A Christmas present from Warren, who had learned my secret all those months ago when we cleaned out the attic.

Newly engaged, we exchanged inner struggles and things we had learned. I talked about my sessions with Prof Frankie and he told me of being bullied as a child. He drew pictures in my mind of his college years and I told of my dance tryouts and life on the road. I made him laugh and tear up for me. This felt like a good bonding time as we went through his stored possessions of clothes, toys, and books.

Interruption

His enormous book collection, from Little Orphan Annie comics to a world atlas I could hardly pick up, impressed me. As we boxed them, we talked about our childhoods and the challenges we had faced. The most impressive thing he said was, "I learned that being teased as a bookworm actually was a badge of honor. Dad told me my love of books would pay off. My different nature wasn't a bad thing but a blessing. My interests would land me a good, steady job." I thought him pretty wise for a kid.

I told him of how I overcame my fear of forgetting my experience in Heaven and what I used as a reminder. Patent leather shoes. The shinier the better. I saw my reflection on the surface even though it was in shadow. Heaven would fade if I didn't keep reliving my time there. I looked at my shoes and my face, although blurry, peered back at me. I was alive. God was real even when I could not see Him. Heaven and my experience were both real. God gave me the present of going there and experiencing Heaven.

I cleaned my shoes, shining them to make the image as clear as possible. Heaven was an elusive place, but I saw it perfectly. I told people what I saw and described all of it the best I could. I brought Heaven into focus to others just as my mind's eye brought my face into focus when I gazed at it from the surface of my shoes.

Warren had hugged me. "Thanks for sharing. I wondered why you wore them almost every day. You're a smart one to come up with that." My love for him grew. He thought of me as smart.

I smiled now, thinking of that day. Most of the books we donated, but many filled the bookcase in his office and another one in his home—our future home.

I finished getting ready. Guests would arrive at any minute. Auntie had left for the day and I baked and cooked. She, Warren, and my future in-laws were coming for dinner. For the last three months, I had learned my way around the kitchen. My mother-in-law-to-be blessed me with her patient teaching.

Tonight, I would show my skills. I prayed again that I hadn't left out anything. I slid the rolls into the hot oven. Those were the only thing I hadn't made myself. The meat sauce had simmered this morning. I set the table hours ago after I made the noodles and assembled the lasagna. The pie cooled on the rack and the lasagna rested on trivets next to the stove.

I placed ice cubes in the glasses. When the doorbell chimed, I opened it to find Warren with a single red rose. "Hello, Jackie. This is for you." I took it and closed my eyes as I breathed in the scent. I opened my eyes and went into his arms. "Thank you!"

He released me and took my hand. I led him into the house. "Come on back to the kitchen. I want to put this lovely rose in a vase."

"It smells terrific in here." He surveyed the room. "You've been busy."

I grinned at him. "I hope everything will taste good." I poured water into the crystal vase I found and placed the rose in it. I buried my nose in the red velvet petals again as I carried it to the dining room—a perfect complement to the table of white linen tablecloth and red napkins. The floral design on the dishes had a touch of red and I used the red goblets. I finished adding the ice and stepped back to take in a good view of the setting. The light above sparkled off the silver utensils. I wanted someday to lay a table as glorious as this one in my own home.

"Everything looks great."

"Thanks."

The doorbell chimed. "Could you get that while I put the ice away and check on the rolls?"

He kissed my cheek then went to the living room. I needed that bolster of courage and love.

Jacquelyn

The dinner went off without a hitch. The companionable atmosphere—perfect. The praises made my cheeks flame. How had I, as a child, gone on stage every night and kept the blush to myself? Did I have a new-found innocence?

Or just a forgiven soul? Something to ponder. Warren said not to be embarrassed when I blushed. It was a battle.

Tonight, friends were giving me a bridal shower. Had someone told me when I sat alone on buses or trains that I would have friends who cared for me, I would have thought they played a mean joke.

Only two weeks and Warren and I will be married. Living in the rehab center all those years ago, I thought my life too despicable for a man like Warren to love and marry me. It took me months to get up the courage to tell him and give him all the wretched details. He lovingly understood and said he loved me more because I'd been through the fire and came out stronger. Warren was an amazing man. I was blessed.

"Jackie, are you ready?" Auntie called from the living room. I grabbed my purse and joined her. I didn't have on my feet the reminder I usually wore, but God saw me and still loved me. I needed to remember that and share His message of love with others.

I found Auntie near the door to the garage. "Don't you look pretty." She wore a dark green box coat suit and green alligator print heels, perfect for the bridal shower. I wore a powder blue party dress with a matching jacket. Today, I wore the same color heels, not my typical black patent leather. I had grown accustomed to and felt comfortable in heels—another example of doing something over and over, it became easy. Reading and memorizing God's Word, speaking to strangers about the Lord, sharing my innermost thoughts and problems with the Lord—all these had become second nature. I slipped on my gloves and followed Auntie to the car.

Fifty or so women mingled in the fellowship hall at our church when we arrived. The place looked amazing. Sunshine yellow and navy blue streamers swirled from the ceiling to the table in the middle where food had been set out. Off to the side, on another table, a large cake sat smiling, its pretty rosettes in yellow and navy. Flowing lettering announced *Blessings to Jacquelyn on Her Special Day*.

Grinning faces and sweet voices greeted us. Love and an occasional hug flowed from these women. Friends, all. Conversation buzzed around the room until Dorothy promised them a game. "But first, let's eat."

We filled our cute yellow party plates with finger foods and grabbed delicate cups of sparkling punch. We sat at tables and enjoyed each other's company and the food.

"Where is Warren taking you for your honeymoon?" Sally, a friend from church, asked.

"The Grand Canyon."

"Oh." She smiled. "Have you been there before?"

I shook my head. "No."

"Are you riding into the canyon?"

"We have reservations but the weather may not let us. It's kind of early in the year."

"Oh. Right. Well, be careful."

"We will. Thanks."

"Why the Grand Canyon?"

"I mentioned it to Warren when we talked about being good enough to get into Heaven. Jesus Christ is the bridge over the gap between my life and Heaven. If I try to get to Heaven on my own merit, it's like trying to jump from the North Rim to the South Rim. Impossible."

"Right. Good picture."

"He wanted to take me there so I could see it for myself."

"You've got yourself a keeper."

"Yes. I do." I smiled at this happily married woman with two adorable kids.

Gretchen asked, "Are you planning to continue working?"

I smiled. I had been asked this question numerous times. "Yes. Warren and I agreed that the shop and my clientele are important. A platform for my purpose to share about the Lord is what is paramount. God may change that later, but for now, I plan on working."

"What a relief. I hoped you'd say that. I didn't want to have to have another person fix my hair. You have a knack and I love listening to you. Because of you, I have a personal relationship with the Lord. I know many who have turned to Christ because of your ministry."

Interruption

My heart overflowed with the grace of the Lord. I smiled and blinked back tears of joy.

Soon, the food had been eaten and the games played. The delicious cake had melted in my mouth and I unwrapped dozens of presents. Ladies helped us load the car's trunk and back seat full of amazing gifts.

Auntie and I headed to Warren's house, where we planned on living after our wedding, to unload. He came out to help as soon as we pulled up.

"Hello, beautiful ladies. Did you come home with treasures?"

I giggled. "We sure did." I opened the trunk.

He whistled. "What did ya do? Rob the stores on Main?"

"Silly. The sweet ladies 'showered' us with gifts. Too bad you couldn't be there."

He kissed my cheek. "I hope you had fun."

"We did. Right, Auntie?"

She beamed at me. "A marvelous time."

I grabbed an armload and followed Warren, his arms full, into the house. After many trips, the dining room held the stash of goodies from our friends and loved ones. Fluffy, dusty rose towels to go with the pink-tiled bathroom, a set of charming dishes for eight, flour sack dish towels for every day of the week from the pastor's wife, cooking utensils, mixing bowls, and doilies crocheted by sweet older ladies, to name a few. We had been flooded with thoughtful and useful gifts.

Interruption

"Jackie, I also have a gift for you." I turned. Warren held a lovely potted iris. I smiled up to his grinning face. "Warren it's beautiful. Thank you."

"You remind me of this iris."

"Why?"

"As you know, here in Colorado these babies grace us in the latter part of spring and into summer. Their bulbs are tucked under the frozen ground and as soon a bit of warmth from the sun makes its presence known, they start to grow. Green blades poke out, surrounding the stalk, acting like a sentry. You have protection around you, God's protection. The blades are the first shoots that point to heaven. Just like, you point to heaven. They surround the real beauty of the stalk that grows tall and proudly blooms a gorgeous flower, also like you.

"This flower pales in comparison to what you saw in Heaven. You also will be extraordinary and changed in Heaven. When I look at an iris, I see a resemblance of you—gorgeous, tall, and proud, pointing others to Jesus and heaven. We can plant this in our garden and there it will procreate. This aspect demonstrates your life. You tell people and they trust Christ and they tell others who trust Christ. So, here babe, is my gift to you to remember who you are. You are wonderfully made and use your gifts and talents that God gave you to lead others to Christ. You are brave, bold, and beautiful and I love you."

The pot, though heavy, I cradled and brushed my cheek against its soft purple petal. With tears streaming and a lump in my throat, I set the pot on the floor and went into his waiting arms. God truly had picked out a perfect man for me to encourage and love me. Jesus had told me so before He sent me back.

Warren kissed me tenderly with love and a promise.

I hugged him. "Good night."

Chapter 24

Faphick

My charge and her groom gazed at each other from across the large room. The once fearful Jackie stood with her head up and smiled with confidence. Her Aunt Sherry held her hand. "Are you ready?"

"Yes."

They would walk together to the front. Human tradition dictated someone to give the bride to the groom. Jackie had no father or mother left on Earth, so her loving aunt filled that void better than most.

Before Jackie and Warren had arrived to announce their engagement, Warren's parents and Jackie's aunt had prayed for this couple. They prayed for this day and had asked Elohim Shomri to put His protection over this assembly, today.

Interruption

Energy from people and Beings charged the room. Only a few times since my creation had I witnessed this atmosphere. Jackie's life, although seemingly normal in human terms, was extraordinary because she listened to the Father's call. He gave her a simple yet mighty task—to speak about Him and tell others of His great love for them. Christ gave this command to His disciples, which translated to every one of His children. Simple, yes. Difficult, absolutely. Beings fight humans who share about the Creator, Almighty God. They want to destroy their witness and if possible their very lives. They tempt, discourage, disparage and cause hurt and disease to His chosen sons and daughters. Jackie chose to accept Him as her Savior and then trust Him to guide and give her strength to share her faith. All His children are called to live this way but too few brave the darkness to spread light to individuals. Jackie's simple obedience brought people to their knees before the throne of God on High. Then they in turn shared the message with others. Each person became a missionary to those around them, giving them hope. God's love and grace flowed out of these people to others in this congregation.

Whaxgum and I weren't the only Guardians. Each soul who had been chosen by God before the foundation of the Earth had their own. All of whom I knew—brave, Valiant ones, chosen for the role of Guardian.

Interruption

People settled into the seats to witness the proceedings. As they chatted among themselves, their Guardians fixed their minds on the protection and encouragement of their charges. I recognized the humans. Jackie now had many friends, as did Warren. Aunt Sherry's and the Wrights' friends also came bearing goodwill and gifts in the form of packages and love.

Those who had met Jackie through her beauty shop numbered to three hundred and thirty-six and they had brought family members of their own. Some of these new friends had previously entered the shop with Brokenness, Anger, Depravity, and Hate, to name a few. After hearing and accepting the message of God's grace and salvation, those evil weights had slipped off and been replaced with God-honoring Beings.

Peace, Goodwill, Love, Honor, Kindness, Gentleness, Meekness, Self-control, Joy, Goodness, Faithfulness, Patience, and others flowed around the room and through one person to another in the light of God's radiance shining on this ceremony. These gifts of the Holy Spirit had been planted in the humans. As the person exercised them, they grew and flowed out in their speech and actions.

Long ago in the Garden of Eden, when only Adam and Eve lived, God on High had ordained marriage. He designed a leaving of family and a cleaving for man and woman, who would then be joined by God in marriage.

Interruption

God on High chose Warren and Jackie for each other and orchestrated their meeting and falling in love.

The Ancient of Days opened the window of Heaven to witness and preside over this event. The melodic angels sang. The Lord of Hosts dispatched thousands of angels to surround the building, keeping out the slime of filthy Beings. This event called for celebration, not war.

I saw the prayers of saints floating up to the Heavenly Father who loved these people with a supreme love. The whispers touched my ears as they lifted. "God go before them. Strengthen this bond. Bless this couple. Enlarge their coasts."

The first strains of human music started the procession of the bridal party. Jackie had called the piece *Canon in D*. Young ladies of different backgrounds possessed a common bond—love for their Creator and this couple. Joy and Happiness swirled, and the women smiled.

Sherry squeezed Jackie's hand. "Shall we?"

Calm flooded Jackie so when the downbeat of the *Wedding March* struck, she easily moved forward in anticipation and Sherry went with her. These two developed a closer relationship than a mother and daughter.

Sweet prayers for the couple wafted upon the air, twirling upward to be heard by the ears of the Most Precious Savior. The chorus of angels, in accord, praised the Lord on High.

Interruption

The minister of the church led the human ceremony. "Who gives this woman to this man?"

Aunt Sherry's voice rang true and strong. "I do." She took Jackie's hand and placed it into Warren's.

The vows got my attention. Jackie and Warren pledged their love, sacrifice, commitment, and fidelity to each other. Never had I heard such heartfelt and somber yet joyful words of adoration and steadfast love binding two humans together. Their souls united in their simple words, "I do."

God's great glory shone down and through the stained glass windows, sparkling off crystal, brass, and metal, bouncing and flitting around the room in rainbows of emerald. The people stilled and gazed all around—even children and babies hushed.

The minister said, "God is shining Himself upon this gathering and this couple. Thank You, Lord!"

Applause erupted and reverberated through the whole building, but nothing like the thunderous answer in Heaven. Praise God!

Children giggled. "Look!"

"Mommy, did you see that?"

As the last clap silenced, the minister said, "Well, Warren, you may kiss your bride."

The long-awaited, passionate, pure kiss brought tears to every person in the gathering.

At the end, the pronouncement we all waited for. "I present to you, Mr. and Mrs. Warren Wright."

The cheer thundered through the room and echoed in Heaven. The God of Sovereign Justice lowered His gavel. Stamping it, Done and Done. "Let no human put it asunder!" His voice shook our dimension. It sounded to all the Beings as mighty thunder. Every Being, Angel, and Valiant One knelt in His Awesome Holiness.

God Almighty had proclaimed.

Faphick

Jackie and Warren celebrated their second year together as husband and wife. As God on High would have it, I, myself, welcomed Fomalt, Guardian of Lorraine Ashley Wright, who came squealing into the world, while Jackie panted, pushed, and released her. Jackie did a tremendous job as the doctor readied to help the baby arrive.

This bundle of joyful innocence came as a blessing from God on High. Warren heard it all from the other room and Whaxgum and I saluted God on High for another one of His exquisite creations making an entrance into the world.

Soon, the cleaned-up baby, bundled tight, and mother were wheeled into a room where rows of beds with partitions kept the semblance of privacy. Warren came in carrying a large teddy bear and kissed Jackie's cheek and took his daughter into his arms.

This warmed my heart. The couple had their work cut out for them on this un-driven road. They would learn, fail, regain hold, try harder, win, lose, and succeed. I couldn't wait for the rest of my time with Jackie and her family and also Whaxgum, and Fomalt. Would God on High grant more children to this couple who loved and feared Him?

The Ancient of Days, God on High, only knows.

THE END

Interruption

Dear Reader,

I am blessed and privileged to have written this story of Jackie and her Guardian Faphick. Although this story is fictional, and strictly from my imagination, there are many 'Jackie's' in the world who have gone through similar struggles. I cried with Jackie as she got her breakthroughs. Those struggles rang true to my life's battles. Do we have Guardian Angels? I believe we do but they may not be with us all the time. I know we are surrounded by things we cannot see. Scripture makes it very clear there are spiritual beings that are good and on God's side and other ones that are fallen and war against God.

I hope this story helps you in some way and points you to God on High, where all comfort comes. I prayed as I wrote this book that these words would impact, enlighten, and encourage you. I prayed for you, not by name, but God knows who you are.

God bless you on your spiritual walk with Him,

Robin

Notes

Names of God used in this story: Lord, God, Father, Jesus, Holy Spirit, Ancient of Days, Lord of Hosts, God on High, Lord on High, Elohim Shomri (God protects), Creator

- Guardian (Valiant Ones) names came from my imagination.

Information on angels and spiritual warfare:

- For a biblical study of angels: Reference John MacArthur's sermon *Grace to You Angels: God's Invisible Army* Pt. 1, 2, 3
- *Armor of God Bible Study* by Priscilla Shirer published by LifeWay Press.
- *War Room* DVD by Stephen Kendrick and Alex Kendrick.

Information on cardiopulmonary resuscitation:

- 1954 James Otis Elam was the first to demonstrate experimentally that cardiopulmonary resuscitation (CPR) was a sound technique. 1956 first closed chest defibrillation and 1965 first portable device. 1956 first mouth-to-mouth resuscitation and military adopted it in 1957. Mid-50s the American Red Cross taught how to perform artificial respiration. Patent leather shoes reflection helps her see and be reminded of all that happened.

- Trains in 1955: I believe they had more stops with more people getting on and off the train, which adds time to travel. I have increased her time from 28 hours to 31.5 hours from Chicago to Grand Junction.
- *You Are My Sunshine*: Oliver Hood wrote the work but did not copyright it, and copyright laws were different in those early years. Paul Rice was a fellow musician friend of Oliver Hood and claimed authorship while selling the rights to Jimmie Davis. Jimmie Davis filed copyright protection, which gave him ownership of the song. "You are my Sunshine," Gene Autry, Bing Crosby, Wayne King, and Johnny Cash, to name a few made it popular from 1939 to 2020 by a two-year-old old named Jaxon. Wikipedia

Please enjoy a glimpse into *Worthless to Priceless*, a historical Christian Fiction story.

Western Colorado 1886

Chapter 1

The form appeared to be a body. Samuel scanned the sky. No birds circled. He rubbed his eyes and refocused. "Giddyap!" His team of horses galloped down the hill in the sagebrush-dotted landscape. Dead or alive, he would not leave the person to become mountain lion or bear food.

"Whoa." The wagon stopped parallel to the figure and his heart raced as he ran. Kneeling, he brushed long dark brown hair away from the sun darkened face. "Land sakes alive! Female—a mere child." Checking for breath, he brought his ear to her mouth and nose. A slight whisper of air brushed his cheek.

He scrutinized her for any protruding bones or other wounds. Soft buckskin covered her completely and nothing seemed blood-stained or amiss. Young, he reckoned. On the cusp of womanhood. "Miss? Can you hear me? Please let me know if you're alive."

A flitter of long lashes answered his plea. Samuel stood and scanned the area for more people, a wagon, or a horse. Nothing. He lifted and carried her to the wagon and hoisted her onto the buckboard's seat, making sure she didn't fall off. He climbed back into the bed and unwound the bedroll. Leaning over, he lifted the frail slip of a gal and rested her on the blankets. He reached for his canteen, raising her head. "Please drink this 'ere water."

After a few sloshes of the precious liquid, she opened her mouth and drank. Her hands clasped his and forced more water. A few gulps and he pulled it away. "Not too much right off."

Her eyes opened and focused on his. He almost tumbled back. Never in his life had he seen a more piercing blue come out of dark skin.

"Feel better? Do you understand me?"

A slight nod.

"Are you alone?"

Another nod.

"Where is your family?"

"Dead." The word croaked out, stunning Samuel.

He bowed his head, took a deep breath, and raised it again to gaze at this forlorn young lady. "I'm headed for Rifle. Be there in a few hours. You're welcome to ride back with me, either sitting up front or if you like, here in the wagon. I can't let you have the water. Don't get me wrong,

I'm planning to share, but we need it to last." Again, he scanned the rough and unforgiving countryside.

"Where were you headed?"

She shook her head and shrugged.

"Can you give me your name?"

A raspy whisper met his ears. "Called Small Flower but my real name is Jenny, Virginia Low."

He tipped his wide-brimmed hat. "Samuel Baunof. Pleased to meet you."

Again, Samuel tilted the canteen to her lips for a brief time. He reached into a pouch and pulled out some jerky. He bit off a piece and slipped it between her dry lips. "Suck on this. The juices will help give you some strength and the salt don't hurt none."

Her cheeks moved as she mulled the leather strip around her tongue. Her eyes never left his face. "I won't hurt you and I'll do my best to get you safely to the doc." She seemed weak and content to ride in the back. Samuel left her and climbed up front into the seat. The Indian name shoved wild thoughts through his brain. It was her story and, he guessed, by all appearances—a terrible one. Abandoned? A runaway? He shook his head to try and rid the jumbled thoughts.

Samuel grabbed the reins of the four-horse team, situated himself, and peered back over his shoulder. Her eyes were closed. Those beautiful eyes would haunt him, never to be forgotten.

Glenwood Springs, Colorado 1887

Chapter 2

Spittle dribbled down her face. Typically, when this happened, Jenny tried to ignore the abusive words and actions. Not giving the townsfolk the satisfaction, she didn't wipe away the thick moisture. Her skin and upbringing made them think of her as a half-breed. No matter what she told them, they believed what they wanted. She knew her heritage and she would never forget her real Ma and Pa.

Again, her stomach growled. Would she ever be full? Back in the Indian camp, she had been fed. She worked hard but was also rewarded with food and lodging. Here, no one would hire her. Scrounging for food through the back alleys barely sustained her.

Once a week in the dark of night, she walked far from the center of town to gardens and farms to dig up beets and potatoes. What would she do when the seasons changed? Fear, hunger, and loneliness were her only companions. She thought this place would be different. She remembered the words of the woman in Rifle a year ago. "I located a family in Glenwood Springs who wants a child." Jenny had made the difficult journey to Glenwood Springs and the promised hope of a family.

Either the woman had misunderstood or someone lied. Soon, it became apparent she wouldn't be a protected and loved child in the home but a slave to work from sunup to past sundown. No hugs or kind words. An abrupt change in the attitude of the master caused her to flee for the second time in her short thirteen years of life.

Her growling stomach brought her back to the present. She rounded another corner in pursuit of something to stave off her suffering. Alone, she wiped the mess from her face and began her search. She heard a door open farther down the alley. To avoid detection, Jenny pressed herself behind a tower of barrels and crates.

When she believed they had gone inside, she crept closer to see what had been tossed out. She needed to move fast to beat the rats. Among the chunked garbage she discovered a huge pile of mush. She wanted to cheer. Instead, she scooped the mess up into a tin plate she had in her rucksack. Quick but silent movements brought her to the other end to make her way to the hiding spot, to eat her find.

Stealth her ally, she wove and darted in and out of shadows around the buildings and occasionally into doorways to stop and listen. An arm snatched her and a hand stifled the scream rising up.

"Shhh. I won't hurt you if you're quiet. I've a job offer, are you interested?"

Jenny nodded. Fear made her feet itch to get away but

the job offer won the battle.

About the Author

Author Photo:
Jamie Herrera Photography
@JamieHerreraPhotography

Robin lives in Sugarmill Woods, Florida with her husband Jimmy and their Belgian Malinois, Kenzi. She and her husband celebrate with an overflowing cup of blessings with seventeen grandchildren. Robin loves company and challenging her young guests to discover the many giraffes in the obvious and hidden nooks and crannies of their home. An award winner for romance and flash fiction, Robin is multi-published in both fiction and non-fiction and has written well over a hundred stories on her blog for children. Two of her novellas are finalists in the 2020 Selah awards.

Books by Robin Densmore Fuson include:
Christian Historical Fiction:
> *Worthless to Priceless*
> Romantic Suspense:
> *Race of Her Heart*

Novellas:
Historical Romance and Suspense:
> *The Dress Shop, Lasso of Love, Gamble on Fate,*
> *Reflection in Glass*

Contemporary Romance: *Etching in the Snow*
Contemporary Romantic Suspense: *Sparkle of Silver*
Romantic Christian Women's Fiction: *The Encounter,*
Restoration
Children grade 3-6 Chapter Book Series:
> *Rosita Valdez and the Giant Sea Turtle,*
> *Rosita Valdez and the Attic's Secrets, Rosita*
> *Valdez and the Spanish Doll*

Visit her at:

Blog, Robin Densmore Fuson:
http://www.robindensmorefuson.com

Blog, Kid Bible Lessons: http://www.kidbiblelessons.com

Amazon Author Page: https://www.amazon.com/Robin-Densmore-Fuson/e/B06XGKVDDV/ref

Twitter: https://twitter.com/RobinLFuson

FaceBook:
https://www.facebook.com/AuthorRobinDensmoreFuson

Instagram:
https://www.instagram.com/robindensmorefuson

Pinterest

Goodreads:
https://www.goodreads.com/author/show/6604786.Robin_Densmore_Fuson

BookBub: https://www.bookbub.com/profile/robin-densmore-fuson

Linkedin: Robin Densmore Fuson | LinkedIn

MeWe

Alignable

YouTube: Robin Densmore Fuson - YouTube

BROKEN YOKE
PUBLISHING

brokenyokepublishing.com

Made in the USA
Columbia, SC
15 July 2021

41922614R00124